JAMIE THOMSON

THE WRONG SIDE OF THE GALAXY

ORCHARD

1 BIRTHDAY BOY

'AAARGHHHH!' bellowed Harry at the top of his lungs. A figure with a heart-shaped face, great big black eyes and a head like a fungus-covered grey turnip had just loomed over him. Harry, terrified at the sight, tried to get up, but he couldn't move. Two more turnip heads followed. Hideous nightmare turnip heads that were clearly not human! Harry began to panic as he struggled harder to get up – why couldn't he move? He looked down – he was lying on a table in the middle of an antiseptic white room. He looked back up at the strange creatures. They were scary for sure, but they also reminded him of something…what was it? Greys! That was it. Greys, those aliens he'd seen in films, the ones that were always abducting people and carrying them off! Ridiculous, of course, I mean, why would aliens come all this way just to carry off…wait a minute!

Harry blinked, staring at the Greys. Come all this way just to carry *him* off... Why would they... Harry gulped. What could they possibly want with a fourteen-year-old boy from Croydon?

'What do you want? Who are you? No, wait, what are you???' he demanded in panicky tones.

At this, the Greys started muttering to each other in voices like croaky mosquito whines. It reminded him of his mate Harvey, who whined and moaned whenever Harry beat him in a game.

One of the Greys tapped a little headset device attached to the side of its head.

'Please lie still, human thing,' it said.

'Don't tell me what to do, you…thing! You turnip thing!' blustered Harry. He was actually rather terrified, but he wasn't going to let them know that.

Another Grey came over to the table. From the way the others immediately hunched over, this one seemed to be in charge. It said something to the one who had spoken to Harry, then pointed with a long snaky finger at a screen on the wall.

Harry stretched his neck so he could see the screen. It was weird, because he was looking past his feet at the screen, but the image on the screen showed the exact same view of his feet, and then him looking at another screen in that. Hundreds of pairs of feet, stretching off to infinity.

He tried looking up, down, to the side. The view on the screen moved too. It showed what he was seeing. But how was that possible – had they wired up his eyes or something? The boss Grey jabbered something, and the one who'd switched his headset on turned to Harry.

'He wants you to close your eyes again, please. We'd like to see more of your Earth memories.'

Harry stared up at the grey-domed alien thing and gulped, unsure what to do, his heart beating like a drum. This was the scariest thing ever!

The boss repeated what he'd said before, his voice sharper now. Harry didn't understand the words, but something about the tone was like when his headmaster ran out of patience.

The Grey who had spoken to Harry looked worried. 'He's getting annoyed...'

Harry blinked. So was *he*! Who did they think they were, carrying him off and treating him like this? Anger and fear filled his heart in equal measure. Unless... His brow knitted in suspicion. It couldn't be real! Surely it was Todd Scarswell – or Scars for short – his archenemy at school, and his gang, dressed up in alien suits and masks.

Either way, he had to do something! Anything. He wrenched at whatever was holding him down but to little effect. It was as if he were wrapped in cling film or something. Some kind of force field, probably, but he was pinned down just as securely as if he'd been chained to the table.

The boss Grey touched his own headset. He was

tut-tutting as he looked at the screen. 'This one's useless,' Harry heard him say. 'It's very stupid and it refuses to show us its memories. Give it another few minutes, and if it still won't cooperate we'll throw it out into space. Really, we'd have better luck with animals.'

'Er... You just switched your translator on, sir. He can hear what you're saying.'

'What? Heh heh.' The boss Grey grinned at him, big dark eyes glistening like saucers. 'My little joke, human thing. Please ignore.'

He switched off his translator, lost the grin, and looked around at the other Greys. You didn't need a translator to tell what it meant when he drew his finger across his throat.

The smaller Grey looked at Harry sadly. 'He's very pleased with your memories,' he lied. 'Nice vivid details.'

Harry was silent for a moment. Surely they weren't going to kill him? He shook his head in disbelief. This couldn't be happening!

'Right, I've had enough of this,' he shouted. 'Is this your idea of a laugh, Scars? Dressing up in

Halloween masks and pratting about?'

Only that wasn't it. He knew it wasn't. The Greys were too short and weedy to pass for Scars and his mates in disguise. Also, when Scars wanted a laugh he didn't put on a mask and pretend to act out a scene from *Doctor Who*, he just shoved your head in the toilet. Simple pleasures.

Incredible as it seemed, this was all really happening. It was his birthday, and the last thing he remembered was leaving the house, Mum's words ringing in his ears. 'Just make sure you're back for dinner, sweetie!' He'd set off...and then...what? That light...being lifted up into the sky in a beam of light? Maybe, yeah, although the memory was fuzzy. It did sound like a classic case of alien kidnapping, come to think of it.

Harry stopped struggling for a minute and tried to think. He couldn't lift his hands off the table, but what about sliding them to the side? He gave it a go, and by stretching his fingers he was able to get them round the edge of the table. While the Greys kept on jabbering at each other, he worked his fingers over to the underside. He could feel something there – an insulated cable tacked snugly along the side.

He dug his fingernails under the edge of the cable. If he could prise it off the surface, maybe he could snap it. Of course, that might only cause a light to go out, or turn the weird TV screen off, but Harry felt better now that he was actually doing something.

He noticed a couple of the Greys looking at him. They hadn't noticed anything yet, but if he did manage to loosen the wire it would be hard to dislodge or break it without them seeing what he was up to.

He had to come up with a way of distracting them. But how? Then it came to him in a flash. The screen.

Somehow – and he had no idea how it was possible – the screen was obviously picking up images from his mind and projecting them for the Greys to watch.

And the Greys were standing around waiting for a show. Maybe they were studying life on Earth or something. If anybody had asked Harry, he couldn't have thought of anything more boring than daily life around where he lived. But if it was what they wanted…

He screwed his eyes tight shut. The teachers at school said he was imaginative. What was it old Moleface had said to him? 'You've an active imagination, Greene, I'll give you that. Trouble is, "daydreamer" isn't a proper job, now is it?'

Oh yes, he could just picture Moleface's fat smirking mug as he'd said that. Then he heard the Greys gabbling in delight and he realised he hadn't just remembered it, he'd projected it onto the screen. They'd actually heard Moleface's words out loud. There was a frantic flurry of rubbery fingers as the Greys all switched their translators to English.

He'd just about got the tips of two fingers under the wire now. He just needed something to keep them occupied. What could he think of that would be really interesting? Then he had a brainwave. What about that computer game he'd been playing with his mate, Harvey? *Astropocalypse*, it was called. There'd been a great bit in their last game where he suckered Harvey's battle cruiser in close to a small asteroid, then used a reverse warp to drop a black hole right in the centre of it. Harvey didn't suspect a thing until his cruiser was sucked out of the sky by the mass of fifty suns all squeezed into a pinhead.

Oh, that was brilliant. It warmed Harry's heart to think of the way Harvey whined and wheedled while he mopped up the rest of his fleet with long-range quantum cannons.

But something was wrong. Instead of looking at the screen, the Greys were muttering to themselves. He heard a guttural click from the chief that the translator turned into an exasperated sigh.

He stopped fumbling with the wire and laid his hands flat on the tabletop. 'What's the matter?' he demanded.

'Um…' The Grey pointed at the screen, and Harry craned his neck. The image of the game was there, but it was very faint and the colours were completely washed out.

'That's not right!' protested Harry. 'The graphics are way better than that. That's a rubbish screen you've got.'

'Imaginary things. Made-up memories. They do not have what we need. They lack…dimension.'

That was a setback. He'd been counting on keeping them gawping at a few episodes of *Doctor*

Who next. But it had to be real memories, did it? Stuff that had actually happened to him personally. All right, then.

He'd just got home after school. The moment he came in through the back door and saw the banner, he'd known exactly what to expect. A long piece of string hung from one cupboard door. There were bits of crayoned paper attached, spelling out H-A-P-P. The rest of the letters were still scattered on the table. Beside the sink was a big bowl full of lumpy white paste, and next to it a clumsily ripped-open pack of cake mix. Dollops of the mix were all over the worktop and the phone was covered with floury fingerprints.

Mum was sitting at the table. She looked up at him, her face covered in flour.

It would have been funny, if her face hadn't been streaked with tears.

'He cancelled, again. I'm sorry, sweetie,' his mum said.

Harry narrowed his eyes in anger. He wanted to stomp up to his room, to tell the whole world to bog off, so he could be alone. He was angry at his dad for not showing up, sure, but worse than that, he was angry at himself for ever thinking that he might. Angry at his mum for giving up so easily, too. She could have gone ahead and baked the cake, put a brave face on it, and then Harry would have made an effort. But no, bang went all the plans and so much for his birthday.

But he didn't stomp off. Instead he went over and put his hand on Mum's shoulder.

'It's OK, Mum,' he said. 'It's not your fault Dad's such a...well, you know.'

His mum looked up at him, put on a pale smile, rested a hand on his...

'Oh, this is good!' the Grey beside him said. 'Lovely vivid colours. Real intensity.'

He patted Harry's arm like a sports coach. There

was an excited jabbering as the show on the screen unfolded. Harry stared at the Greys. Their long, bony fingers and strange round bodies filled him with horrified terror. He couldn't take this much longer, he had to do something. He let a corner of his mind cycle through his memories, keeping the alien creatures distracted, whilst he concentrated on working the wire loose enough. He could get all his fingers under it now. Nearly there…

Harry was showing them his memory of a terrible row between his mum and dad and how Harry had left them to it in disgust. An excited cheer rose from the Greys as they watched him storming out of the door on screen. Actually, it was really a sort of buzzing howl that the translator turned into a cheer.

'Maybe you should get some popcorn, you vegetable heads!' shouted Harry. And with that he wrenched the cable loose.

There was a soft crackle of sparks and the table slowly sank a couple of feet like a dentist's chair. That was all.

The Greys turned on him. He saw the chief Grey

pulling a thin rod of blue metal from a scabbard at his belt.

'Whoops,' said Harry.

And that's when the room exploded.

2 UP ABOVE THE WORLD SO HIGH

IT was as if somebody had put a jet engine under the floor and revved it up to maximum. A wind tore through the room with enough force to make the metal table lurch. If he hadn't been held down by the force field, he would have gone flying. The Greys were simply ripped off their feet and vanished, flung up out of his line of sight by the unstoppable rush of air.

The Grey who had been talking to him managed to grab hold of the table. Harry could see his mouth moving, but with the hurricane raging all around them it was impossible to hear a thing.

The Grey's rubbery fingers were clamped tight on the table, but the wind was too strong. He slid along the side of the table, fighting for life every inch of the way. At the top he clung on for a moment, his face hanging there right next to Harry's.

'Leptira battle cruiser,' came the voice of the translator over the shriek of escaping air. 'Sneak attack. We—'

And then he was gone. Wiped away like a dead bug on a car windscreen. The wind was dying down, but that wasn't a good thing. It was dying down because it had carried away all the air.

Harry took huge gulps into his lungs but it wasn't doing any good. His heart was hammering away inside his chest and he was getting dizzy and light-headed. Light-headed enough not to even mind dying on an alien spaceship. He was just annoyed that he never got the chance to tell his dad to bog off for bailing on him and his mum. His poor mum.

He raised his hand to swipe angrily at empty air. That's when he realised the force field had switched off. Rolling from the table, he staggered to his feet and found himself staring out into space.

There was another ship hanging out there in the blackness. From the red glow around the tubes at its prow, it was a fair bet those tubes were what had just blown a gaping hole in the hull.

The Greys were all strung out there in a line, lifeless, turning slowly in the vacuum like leaves thrown across a pond. The nearest one, drifting out from the ship behind the rest, he guessed must be 'his' Grey. The one who'd looked so imploringly at him with those big round eyes. Harry almost felt sorry for him. Not so much for the others, though.

Especially not the boss.

He sucked in a breath and tasted the antiseptic air of the ship. Acrid as it was, he couldn't imagine anything sweeter because it meant the atmosphere was coming back. Something must have plugged the gash in the hull. Something like, he guessed, the force field the Greys had used to snare him in the first place.

Now that the air was back, he could hear a soft insistent chiming like the warning some cars give when the door isn't closed. It was coming from a speaker in the ceiling. It sounded too little and too late, but it meant that he wasn't alone on the ship. Somebody had to have set that alarm going and switched on the force field.

'Anyone hear me?' he called.

The speaker fizzed and crackled, and it took him a second to realise that it wasn't just static. It was a language. Stumbling towards the door in frustration, he trod on one of the translator headsets. He snatched it up and hooked it around his ear. Luckily it was still set to translate to English.

'...system failure,' the voice on the loudspeaker was saying. 'Life support at seventy-one per cent. Fusion Reactor at thirty per cent. Shields at forty—'

'Weapons, you idiot!' screamed Harry. 'Hasn't this ship got any laser cannons and whatnot? Fire back at them!'

'Weapons at...' There was an unbearable pause. '...six per cent. Analysis suggests first Leptira attack was designed to disable offensive capability.'

There was something about the droning, clipboardy tone. Like his computer science teacher. 'Don't tell me you're a robot.'

There was no reply. Of course. 'Are you a robot?' said Harry.

'Ship's computer functioning at eighty-two per cent,' replied the voice, sniffily.

Harry cast another glance out into space. The other ship had moved nearer. Was it his imagination, or had the glow in its torpedo tubes got brighter?

'Leptira weapons array recharging,' said the computer. 'Estimate ninety-eight seconds before they fire again.'

'How many hits can we take?'

The computer replied to that perkily enough: 'A number less than one.'

Harry blinked. He had to do something! He stabbed blindly at the door. He couldn't see a button or sensor, but it shot open and he wasted no more time. Running down a dimly red-lit corridor, he called out to the computer: 'Seal that door in case the force field goes down. What about propulsion? Can we outrun them?'

He had to admit that part of him was almost enjoying this. It was just like a game of *Astropocalypse*, as far as the adrenaline rush was concerned.

'Impulse drive insufficient for evasion,' announced the computer. 'Maximum speed of Leptira Type II battle cruiser exceeds ours by factor of five.'

Harry swallowed. OK, maybe with the Xbox you didn't usually get that sick feeling of imminent searing death. Harry began to think furiously, trying to find a way out.

'What about warp? Hyperspace. Can't we just jump?' he said.

'Quantum Interstitial Drive is offline.'

'Bring it online! Get us out of here!'

'Quantum Interstitial Drive will take one hundred and thirty seconds to energise,' the computer replied, adding calmly: 'Reactor now at twenty-eight per cent. To energise quantum drive, shields must be powered down.'

'Do it.' That was a no-brainer. If the other ship could take them out with one shot anyway, the shields were a waste of time.

'Quantum drive initialising. Leptira vessel will be ready to fire in eighty-three seconds. Eighty-two seconds… Eighty-one seconds… Eighty…'

'All right, I get it, stop counting down!' barked Harry.

'Sorreee!' said the computer.

A sarcastic alien computer? Really? But Harry didn't have time to think about that.

An idea came to him. 'If there's any energy to spare, put it into – what did you call it? Impulse drive. Let's at least get moving.'

'You wish to leave orbit?'

'Yes. No, go lower.'

'Yes/No! Make up your mind!' snapped the computer.

'Lower!' said Harry. Maybe they wouldn't expect that. 'Where's the bridge?'

'Take elevator to upper deck,' said the computer.

That small room at the end of the corridor just had to be the elevator. He dashed inside. There were no buttons, but there was a recessed glass panel on the wall. Harry swept his hand up it, like swiping photos on a smartphone, and the doors slid shut. His stomach flipped as the elevator sped upwards.

He wondered if all the entire crew had been watching his 'show', and that they'd all been killed. Probably so, if the computer was running things now. He was on his own.

A nasty thought struck him. 'What happens if we go to warp with that hole in the side?'

'Seventy-five per cent probability of quantum depressurisation,' said the computer.

'What does that mean?'

The elevator stopped and the doors swept open.

'The entire substance of the ship and its occupants would be converted to dark matter,' explained the computer.

Quantum depressurisation: there'd be no coming back from that. But a second blast from the whatever-they-were-called would have the same effect, and that was a dead certainty. Harry would have to take his chances on that all-important twenty-five per cent gap. Or hope that the computer had got it wrong.

He came out on a small circular observation gallery overlooking what might be the control room. Leaning over the balustrade, he could see panels of winking lights directly beneath, and a blue glow from a screen running right around the wall.

The domed ceiling here was transparent, giving him a view of the enemy cruiser as it hove into view overhead. Harry stared in awe. If all those

observation ports were built to anything like human scale, the damned thing was as big as an office block! Its weapon tube was pulsing with white heat now. Less than one hit, the computer had said. He could believe it.

He wondered if, behind those shiny black portholes, alien eyes were watching. Somehow he guessed the Leptira would be a lot less humanoid than the Greys. More the sort of aliens you'd enjoy blowing to slimy chunks with a blaster.

A face appeared right above him. One of the dead Greys, drifting in space, bumped against the glass. Harry jumped back in shock, his legs hitting the balustrade that ran around the gallery. It was designed to be at a safe height for the Greys, but all of them were at least a foot shorter than him. His arms shot out but there was nothing to hold onto. He fell fifteen feet to the floor below, slamming into a chair which spun, flinging him against a panel of dials and monitors. His forehead scraped against metal, blood washed into his eyes, and he fought against blacking out.

'How long now?' he said thickly. Then he noticed

his translator had been dislodged in the fall. He scrambled across, wedged it back on his ear, and repeated the question.

'Quantum drive will be online in fifty-seven seconds.'

That meant less than ten seconds before the enemy ship was ready to blow them out of the sky. Harry looked up at the screen and gasped. It was the Earth, and it filled the screen. They must be entering the atmosphere.

Harry had a sudden flash of inspiration. Sometimes down on the towpath by the canal, he and Harvey would skim stones over the water. Could you do that same trick with an eight hundred ton spaceship on the upper layer of the atmosphere?

Only a few seconds to go. It was worth a try. 'Pull up,' he told the computer, 'sharp as you can. Now!'

Harry felt the floor slide away and he dropped with a crash into the wall. The screen darkened as the view spun away from Earth and out into deep space.

Then there was a second, deeper shudder and

he had to hang on for dear life as the ship went tumbling end over end, the blue disc of the Earth looking smaller each time it swept by on the screen. There was a dull roar far down in the lower decks, and at the same time about half the lights in the control room went out.

The other ship must have fired, but thanks to skimming off the atmosphere they'd only caught a glancing blow. No telling how much damage it had done, but at least they were in one piece for now.

'Less than one shot, you said!' laughed Harry hysterically. 'Well, we took one and we're still here!'

There was no reply. This time the buzz from the speaker really was just static. Harry felt real terror. Death seemed certain. He thought of the Greys, sucked out to drift like debris in space, millions of miles from home. They must have had families, but they'd never know what happened to them.

'The drive,' said the speaker.

'Yes!' Harry felt a spurt of hope. 'How long now?'

'The drive... Quantum drive.' That shot had done some serious damage to the computer.

'As soon as it's online, go to warp,' said Harry,

desperately hoping the computer could keep it together long enough.

The screen filled with what looked like the peak of a mountain rising into view. Harry's heart sank. It was the alien battle cruiser. Despite their bounce off the atmosphere, the Leptira had caught up to them in no time. The glow in the gun tube showed it was charging up to fire, and there'd be no clever evasive manoeuvre this time. They were crippled, hanging in space waiting to die.

'Quantum drive requires manual initialisation,' said the computer.

'You want me to press something? Where? What?' said Harry.

'No hyperspace course available,' said the computer.

'Never mind that.'

That gun was pulsing again. The ship was right on top of them. 'The drive…' The computer sounded like his granddad looking for the spectacles that were on his head all along. 'Quantum drive requires…'

'Manual whatsit!' screamed Harry. 'I know! Show me what button to press!'

Every single light in the cabin went out. All the consoles were dead. Harry slumped against a chair. It was hopeless. The computer had had its brains blown out and now the power had gone off. He stared into the fiery white mouth of the Leptira cannon and knew it was hopeless.

Then one light came on. Just one button, on the panel in front of him. For a second he couldn't think, couldn't act. Then he lunged for it. The Leptira fired. Harry hit the button. And space turned inside out.

3 · VANISHING POINT

HARRY put out a hand to steady himself against the elevator door. The door helpfully swished open and he stumbled into the corridor.

He couldn't remember a thing after the jump to hyperspace. It felt like he'd been out cold for quite a while. The cut on his head had had time to dry, the blood now sticky like old jam that'd been left in a cupboard for weeks. And he was so thirsty that he had to peel his tongue off the roof of his mouth like a piece of Velcro.

But he was alive. And the ship was still in one piece. You had to take the glass-half-full view of things, that's what his mum always said.

What would his mum do when he didn't come home? She'd call Harvey's parents first. They wouldn't know, of course. Then the school – even less of a clue! Then the police... Harry smiled to himself. Maybe they were all looking for him right now! Then he frowned. They'd never find him, obviously. How was he going to get back to Earth, even, let alone get back in time for his ruined birthday dinner?

Well, he'd have to worry about that later. For now, water was the first thing he had to take care of.

His legs felt wobbly. He couldn't tell if that was because of being knocked out or a simple case of dehydration. Supporting himself with one hand on the wall, he headed along the corridor. It ran straight ahead, with other corridors curving off every now and then. The ship was designed like a wheel, as far as he'd been able to tell, and he was now in one of the spokes.

'Anyone there?' he called.

Silence. The computer must have fried its last circuit telling him which button to press. Annoyed as he had been by its prissy sarcasm, it was much worse having no one to talk to at all.

Maybe he could send out a distress signal. He didn't even know Morse code, let alone the alien signal for 'SOS', but if he just broadcast a message into space, surely a Grey ship could trace it back. But what would the crew of a rescue ship think when they found him alone on the ship? Would they take him home to Earth, or would they strap him back in front of a telepathy screen and bring out the metal probes? Or would they decide he was the killer and shoot him on the spot?

There was the hole in the hull, though. They'd see he couldn't have possibly done that. It was the other aliens – what had the Grey called them? The Leptira. 'It was a surprise attack by the Leptira,' he could tell them.

It would be a lot easier to think without the ringing in his ears and the dull throb where he'd whacked his head. But he had to try something or he'd die of thirst, alone in the depths of space. Just then, he caught sight of a cabinet with a large, fat bottle on top of it just a little further down the corridor. It was so perfect and so unexpected that he just stood there blinking stupidly at it for a couple of seconds before his brain accepted that, yes, it really was a water cooler. Just like you'd find in an office back on Earth. He almost laughed for joy.

He grabbed a cup, filled it with water and raised it to his lips.

But then a nagging doubt struck him. People in a shipwreck couldn't drink seawater. It would drive them mad or poison them or something. And that was just because of the salt. So what about *alien* water?

But the Greys breathed air, after all, even if it did smell a little like a doctor's clinic. And of all the planets they could go and kidnap people from, they had chosen to come to Earth. Why was that? Maybe it was because their own planet was similar.

He held the cup inches from his lips. What should he do? It was like having a voice in each ear. It's safe. It's deadly.
Drink. Don't drink.

'If I don't drink, I'll die anyway.'

Saying it out loud like that helped to convince him. But speaking aloud also made him realise how isolated he was. Far, far out beyond the moon, probably. His eyes welled up with tears.

He felt so alone.

Or was he alone? A tingle ran up the back of his neck and he spun around. He was just in time to catch a flutter of movement at the end of one of the curving corridors.

A light in the ceiling flared and went out, plunging that part of the corridor into darkness. Harry blinked. He must have noticed the bulb flickering just before it died. That was the 'movement' that had caught his eye. The sense of being watched hadn't gone away, but he forced it out of his mind. Who could possibly be watching him? All the Greys had been sucked out of the ship like bugs into a vacuum cleaner, hadn't they?

'I'm going off my head with thirst is what it is,' he announced.

The cup was still in his hand. He steeled himself and gulped some of it back.

'Aargh!'

He grabbed his throat. It wasn't poison – it was acid! He could feel the bubbles fizzing in his mouth as it dissolved his tongue. Frantically he spat out the liquid that hadn't already gone down his throat.

Then he stopped as the first wave of panic passed and he had time to think. There was no actual pain in his mouth. His tongue was still in one piece – and not only that, it didn't taste like a stale sock any more. The only sensation was cool and wonderfully refreshing.

He shoved the cup back under the spigot and refilled it. This time he gave the liquid a closer look. There were little bubbles rising through it.

'It's fizzy water, that's all,' he realised, feeling a complete idiot. Just as well there was nobody around to see him shrieking and clutching at his throat and spitting all over the place because he'd been driven into a girly panic by a mouthful of sparkling water.

He took a proper gulp, and another. It tasted so good. Funny how a few mouthfuls of good clean water were enough to raise the spirits. And suddenly he found himself doubled up with laughter at his own idiocy, the bubbles shooting painfully up his nose as he spluttered water all down his front.

He was still chuckling when he heard another peal of laughter ring out behind him.

This time he whirled quick enough to get a

glimpse of running feet disappearing around the curve in the corridor. He exploded into action, flinging himself after the retreating figure. If there was at least one Grey left alive, maybe that meant a chance of steering the ship back to Earth.

The curving corridor hid whoever it was from view, but he could hear their running footsteps and he knew he was gaining on them.

He saw the flash of slender legs as the figure darted down one of the cross-cutting passageways. The sound of running feet was followed by a soft thud and then silence. Maybe it was a trap. He would turn the corner to find himself face to face with a bunch of Leptira – whatever they looked like – armed with ray guns, and a barrage of laser fire would reduce him to a pile of smoking bones with a little bit of red barbecued flesh sticking to them. But he'd had enough of running and hiding. He charged on.

He skidded to a halt at the intersection of the corridors, all pumped up to give a blood-curdling yell and pile into whoever was waiting there. But instead his jaw fell open in astonishment.

It wasn't a Leptira. It wasn't a Grey. The figure he'd been chasing had blue skin with a patterning of large violet freckles. And—

'You're a girl!' gasped Harry.

She was facing him in a crouch. It looked as if she'd leaped in a forward roll and was just getting to her feet. He was on the point of wondering why when he took a step towards her and found himself suddenly flailing around in midair, feet kicking at nothing. He was floating, weightless, a few feet off the floor.

The girl straightened up and came closer. Harry noticed that she had two sets of eyelids – one regular pair, and another that closed sideways over golden eyes like a cat's. She didn't look anything like the Greys. They were as ugly as month-old prunes, but this blue girl looked more like a character in an animated movie. Weird, but sort of stylishly weird.

'What have you done to me?' he demanded.

She seemed surprised that she could understand him until she noticed the translator.

'I switched off the gravity tile,' she said, pointing to a small fuse box that he hadn't noticed at the junction of the corridor.

'Well, switch it back on!'

He made a grab for her, but the movement only sent him spinning round helplessly in the air. How did astronauts get around the space station? They pulled themselves along like in a jungle gym. He extended a hand but the wall was too far to reach, and again he just started rotating where he hung.

He felt himself going red with humiliation, but at least the girl wasn't laughing at him. She was just standing with her hands on her hips, looking at him with an utterly amazed expression, like you might have if you saw a squirrel dancing the tango on your washing line.

'The more you struggle'

He continued to swing around.

'the more you're going to keep spinning.'

Wait – now she was standing at the junction behind him? Harry was getting dizzy, but not dizzy enough to be seeing double. He craned his neck – slowly, though, so as not to set himself off spinning again.

'There are two of you!' he said.

'No. There's one of'

'me and there's one of'

'her.'

They looked identical. The same light blue skin, huge golden eyes under a domed forehead, hair like a curtain of tiny black beads, perfect button noses that flared in haughty disdain as they watched him. Even the dark green jumpsuits were the same. Everything an exact copy except for a small symbol that he noticed in the hollow of their throats.

What were those symbols? Tattoos, or – ?

'Are those bar codes?' he said.

They sighed – exasperated, impatient and disapproving sighs. Alien blue-skinned freaks they might be, but they were definitely girls, all right.

'I've seen some pretty dumb fashion trends,' said Harry, 'but I never thought of wearing a barcode. What does it say if you swipe it? Two for the price of one?'

The blue girls frowned.

'You think'

'you're funny. But'

'you're a very inferior—'

'Wait, I've got it,' said Harry. 'You two are clones, right?'

Exactly in unison, like dancers, they folded their arms and shifted their weight indignantly onto one hip.

'That is'

'a question'

'you just'

'don't'

'ask.'

'That means you are! I bet you've got telepathy and all. That's why you keep finishing each other's sentences.'

'I don't finish'

'her sentences. She starts'

'mine.'

'Oh, look, this is all making my head spin. Even if I wasn't dangling in midair, I mean. Will one of you just fix the gravity thingy so I can get down

from here?'

'Can't,' said one of the girls.

Harry gritted his teeth. 'Why?'

'You might be'

'angry, perhaps even'

'dangerous.'

'I'm not angry!' shouted Harry at the top of his lungs, causing the blue girls to blink with both sets of eyelids and take steps backwards.

Suddenly he noticed that the ringing in his ears had stopped at last. It had been going on for so long that he had forgotten all about it, but he noticed now that it had gone.

'How about that?' he said to the girls. 'Yelling at you pair of weirdos has cleared that noise in my ears.'

'That wasn't'

'in your ears. It was'

'the hyperspace drive. It finally'

'ran out of power.'

They both turned and ran off in different directions without another word.

'Hey, wait!' called Harry. But they were gone.

Harry assessed the situation. The first thing was to get out of the weightless zone. He couldn't reach the walls, but the corridor was low, built to the tiny stature of the Greys. By swinging around his centre of gravity he was able to stretch his toes up to the ceiling. A light kick was enough to propel him forwards a couple of feet. His shoulders drifted over the next tile, where the gravity field was still on, and the next moment he was flipped head over heels to land smack in the middle of the floor. Getting to his feet, he set off to look for the two alien girls.

He didn't have to go far. They were standing in the outermost corridor, the one that must curve right around the rim of the wheelship. There was a long observation window and the girls had their faces pressed up to the glass, staring out. He could tell by their expressions that something was wrong.

'What can you see?' He joined them at the window. 'What's up? There's nothing out there.'

He'd always imagined outer space to be filled with stars everywhere you looked. One time when he was small, he'd gone fishing with his dad in the Lake District, and at night there were so many diamond-hard points of light in the sky – far more than you'd ever see in the town after dark – that it was impossible to count them. Literally. His dad said there were more stars than grains of sand in the Sahara, and although Harry didn't see how that was possible, he still knew there were millions. That was the last time he'd seen his dad.

But all he could see now was dead black space.

'Where are all the stars?' he said.

'They're in the Milky Way,' said the nearer girl.

'Obviously. Duh.' Harry scowled at her. 'But why can't we see them, then?'

'Because the Milky Way is over there,' said the other girl.

He turned his head in the direction she was pointing. There, far off in the black void of space, was the unmistakable shape of the galaxy – a small oval disc of glittering white pinpricks. Numb with shock, Harry raised his hand towards it. His fingers slid up over the cold glass. When he spread them, they covered most of the Milky Way. A whole galaxy under the palm of his hand.

'The quantum drive is only supposed to be used for a couple of minutes at a time,' one of the girls was saying.

'But without the computer we didn't have any way to shut it down,' added her twin.

Harry couldn't get his head around it. 'So...what? What are you saying?'

'The ship's been in hyperspace all this time, until the quantum drive ran out of fuel just now.'

The other girl nodded. 'Instead of a jump of the usual trillion miles or so, we've gone a quintillion miles.'

'You're making this up. Are those even real numbers?'

'See for yourself.'

They both pointed.

Harry let his hand drop to his side. That was the entire galaxy, exactly like it looked in books! And yet it was as tiny as a party balloon that somebody had released to go soaring up and up into the clouds.

'So we've finally come to a stop but we're, like, a million light years out from the edge of the galaxy, is that it?'

'Oh, no.' The girls looked at each other out of the corners of their huge bright eyes and hid condescending smiles.

'I'm glad you can see the funny side of this,' Harry fumed. 'What's the joke?'

'Only your lack of astronavigation skills. We haven't come to a halt. Why would we? The fuel's all gone, but that doesn't mean the ship loses its forward momentum.'

'We're still travelling away from the galaxy at about a thousand miles a second.'

'And since we're out of fuel…'

Harry felt an unbearable weight settling on his shoulders.

'…there's no way we can stop.'

They both looked at him and spoke in unison. 'We'll keep on going out into space for ever and ever.'

4 CRUMBS

'**YOU** really are the most'
  'ill-tempered'
  'crude and'
  'exasperating'
  'alien I've ever met.'

Harry scowled, looking from one to the other. They finished each other's sentences so fast that his head was spinning. They had found the ship's canteen. There were rows of tables and trays of cutlery, all infant school-sized to fit the Greys. But, to Harry's dismay, the big cabinet at the back of the canteen that looked like it had been some sort of food dispenser had been smashed open and the contents all eaten.

The two girls sat down perkily at a table and waited, like they expected him to dish them up a meal. Harry sighed to himself. He wasn't their servant, for goodness' sake!

He jabbed a finger at them. 'Anyway, before you go calling anyone an alien, I'm not the one who was born in a vat and looks like a Smurf, all right? And why'd you break the vending machine if you're so hungry?'

He turned over the broken plastic casing of the machine, which was lying on the floor, and held up a couple of crumpled silver wrappers

that still had a few crumbs of something honeyish and sticky on them. The girls sniffed and narrowed their inner set of eyelids, the ones that closed side to side. 'We didn't' 'break anything.' 'Who did, then? There's only us on board.' Harry threw the wrappers down. 'What are we supposed to live off? Each other?'

They made a trilling sound, a bit like a cat

screeching. Harry's headset couldn't cope with it. After a brief pause, a synthesised voice in his ears said, 'A type of scornful laughter unique to the inhabitants of the planet Yureshto.'

Scornful laughter, eh? Harry had a feeling he would get to be very familiar with that sound. He might as well be back in the playground back home – but instead of Scars's older sister and her gang, it was two mad alien manga twins. Oh, and he was in a spaceship. On the other side of the galaxy…the wrong side of the galaxy.

'Anyway,' said Harry, 'Have you two got names?'

'Of course. I am Alpha and she is Beta. You may call us Alph and Bet.'

'Ah, well, OK then, you should have said. Alph and Bet it is.'

'And what's your name?' demanded Alph.

'Harry. Well, Henry.'

'Which?'

'Henry.'

'So why did you say Harry?'

'It's short for Henry.'

She blinked disturbingly with both sets of eyelids.

'No, it's not.'

'It's the same,' said Bet.

'Never mind!' Harry said. 'What's the point of arguing about names when we're starving to death?'

'It's a big ship,' said Alph.

'What's that got to do with anything?' said Harry.

'There'll be another food dispenser somewhere,' said Bet.

'Great – where, though?' said Harry.

'Don't know,'

'we ask and'

'they bring it to us,'

'coz we're royalty,' said the girls.

'Hah! Don't make me laugh!' said Harry.

The girls exchanged a look.

'Why would we make you laugh?' said Bet.

'Now, be a good boy, run along and get us our dinner,' finished Alph.

Harry groaned. Only six hours since he'd been dragged off into outer space and already he had two girls bossing him about. 'Anyway, it's my birthday – you should be getting me dinner,' he muttered.

'What is that, what you just said?' said Bet.

'You know, birthdays... "Happy birthday to me, happy birthday to me, happy birthday dear Harry—"'

'OMG!' shrieked Bet in delight (or so the translator said). 'Listen to that, Alph. It's the Merry Hatching Day song.'

'It's such a stupid little tune, it's probably sung the whole galaxy over,' said Alph.

'Clones hatch from eggs, do they?' said Harry.

'No!' laughed Bet. 'It's sort of a tank, really, with tubes and pumps—'

'Don't tell him all about us!' Alph whirled around angrily. 'He's not our friend. He's an unwashed, uncouth alien thing from a backward planet.'

'Hey, sitting right here,' said Harry with a snort of laughter.

'I just thought—' said Bet.

'I know,' said Alph. 'But what's the point? Why get to know each other when we'll be dead in a couple of weeks, anyway?'

Harry shook his head at that. That was giving up, that was. Just like his dad, who'd given up on him and Mum and left. But Harry wasn't like his dad.

He wasn't going to give up.

'If I go down, I'm going to go down fighting,' he told Alph.

After a pause, Bet also turned to her twin. 'Me too,' she said.

The twins stared at each other. Silence reigned. To break it, Harry said, 'OK, then. So how is it you're here?'

'Pardon?' they both said, turning back to face him.

'Well, you're from the planet Yureshto, right?'

'How do you know that?' said Alph suspiciously.

'Translator told me. So here's these two Yureshtian – Yureshtese? – whatever, these two blue manga girls on a spaceship with a bunch of little grey prune faces. What's the deal? You said they fed you. Why?'

'We're not actually from Yureshto. Though it's true our species does live there.'

'Don't tell him.'

'Alph, we have to cooperate. We're all in this together.'

Harry snapped his fingers. 'Oh, I got it. They

cloned you. The Greys. They were the ones who grew you in a tank or whatever.'

'We already explained—' began Alph.

'That's why they kidnap people,' said Bet. It was the first time Harry had heard her interrupt her twin rather than just finishing a sentence. 'They collect a specimen of a new species, then they take a DNA sample and so on and create clones. Species from all over the galaxy, in fact. And they bring up the clones on Canus Prime – that's the Greys' Homeworld – using memory tapes collected from each planet so that the clone will know how to blend in.'

'You're saying they wanted to record that stuff to teach other clones what life is like on Earth?'

Bet nodded. 'They train the clones so they'll fit in when they put them back on their planet of origin. That's where we were going – to Yureshto, to drop us off.'

'OK, and all, but…you know…why?' asked Harry.

'Spies. The clones have implants that send everything they learn back to the Greys. Most of it is useless, but there's always a nugget or two of information here and there that they can sell to – well, whoever will buy it, really. Scientists. Corporations, governments. Even warlike aliens like the Leptira who are always looking for places to invade.'

'Huh.' Harry thought it sounded like a cheap sci-fi movie – though, come to think, if it was, he'd probably go and see it. 'So they wanted my DNA so they could make a bunch of Harry Greene clones, eh?'

'Obviously they would have thrown you back when they realised what a poor specimen of your species you were,' said Alph.

'Right, very funny,' said Harry with a sigh. 'Birthdays are supposed to be fun. Party hats and presents. Games and that. Instead I'm having one of the worst days of my life.'

They both laughed.

'What's so funny?' said Harry, scowling at them.

'One of the worst days?' said Alph. 'Surely this must'

'be the worst day ever!' said Bet.

'Getting kidnapped by aliens and lost in intergalactic space? That's only mediumly rubbish compared to some days.' Harry shrugged. 'You wouldn't know. You're clones.'

'What does that mean?' said Bet, puzzled.

'It means you haven't got a family to let you down.'

'I've got'

'me.'

'Here, I'll show you my lot.' Harry reached into his pocket. Then he jumped up, doing a sort of frantic dance as he patted frantically at his other pockets.

'Whatever's the matter?' said Bet.

'It's gone. My phone…'

'This far out, I don't think there'll be any coverage,' sighed Alph.

'For the photos of my folks, you blue twerp!' said Harry.

'You probably dropped it,' said Bet hurriedly. 'When the Greys tractor-beamed you aboard.'

Harry shook his head. 'No, I'd have noticed. I reckon it was still in my pocket on the bridge. Then I hit my head, we went to warp speed, I blacked out...' He shook his head, annoyed. 'It's no good, I can't remember when I had it last.' Harry walked over to the canteen water cooler and drew himself a cup full of fizzy water, trying to recall things.

Suddenly, there was a loud thump.

'What was that?' said Bet, eyes going so wide they were like gold CDs in her head.

'It came from the cabin next door,' said Alph.

Harry leaped to his feet. 'There's someone else on board!'

HARRY stepped out into the corridor, the girls just behind him. The clone twins pointed at the door opposite.

'That'

'one,' they said.

Harry waved a hand. The door slid open with a hiss.

'Go ahead, take'

'a look. We're'

'right behind you,' said the girls.

'Who's there?' called Harry from the doorway. No answer.

The room had a big domed transparent ceiling. Some kind of observation chamber, no doubt. Beyond the dome, a vast blackness stretched away in all directions. Harry tried not to think about that. Around the edge of the circular room was a raised platform. And – there! He could just see a pair of feet, standing on the observation gallery to the left, the rest of the figure hidden by the door lintel. Harry's brow furrowed. There was something odd about those feet. They were improbably long. And floppy.

Wait a minute, Harry thought to himself. *They can't be…clown feet, can they? A clown? On a spaceship?*

He stepped forward for a better look. Suddenly there was a buzzing sound and a flash of light, blinding him for the briefest of moments. When he recovered, he saw a thin, spindly human, looking down at him from the gallery. He was dressed in a suit, a normal modern-day Earth suit. Except that it was bright red. And the tie was yellow. And the feet seemed…normal enough. Well, perhaps a little large, but certainly not clown feet. Big feet, but not clown feet. Had it been his imagination? The suit colours, though – they were a bit clowny. What was going on?

'Greetings, my friends. No doubt you are wondering—' began the figure.

'Who are you?' interrupted Harry, trying to sound tough and in charge.

The figure paused for a moment, unsure. Harry sized it up. It was clearly human but reassuringly scrawny and weak-looking. Still, Harry couldn't afford to take any chances. He held up his hand to show that he was carrying a...cup of fizzy water. *Idiot!* he thought to himself. He clenched his other hand into a fist and raised it menacingly.

The figure spoke nervously. 'I am...errr...Rib... errr...Rib...Ribshack Gaggenow. You may call me Gaggenow.'

'Ribshack Gaggenow? What kind of name is that?' said Harry disbelievingly.

Gaggenow just shrugged. Harry stared at him, frowning. Something wasn't right. The shape of the face, the configuration of the limbs. And those feet…

'You're not human, are you?' he said.

'Yes, yes, I am. I was born on Earth just like you were,' said Gaggenow.

'Uh huh. And where are you from, then?' demanded Harry.

'I hail from the planet Earth, of course, my friend, as I said. That is why I have such a common Earth name,' said Gaggenow.

'Common Earth name? You have to be kidding,' retorted Harry. 'I mean, Ribshack, right? That's, like, a restaurant or something.'

'Is it indeed, what a coincidence,' said Gaggenow breezily.

Harry stared at him. 'Yeah, well, nobody gets called Ribshack, and certainly not as a first name – and Gaggenow…that's…what kind of name is that?'

Gaggenow shifted uncomfortably on his large feet. A little burst of light flashed off one of his improbably sized shoes. *That was weird*, thought Harry to himself.

'Anyway,' said Harry, 'I meant, where on Earth are you from. You know, like, where were you born?'

'Oh, I see, of course! Yes, umm…in…ahh…' Gaggenow suddenly fell silent. He looked at the back of his hand, as if fascinated by something he saw there. Then he looked up at the empty black infinity beyond the observation dome and pointed at it lazily.

'Looks like we're lost, wouldn't you say, young man?' he said.

Harry shook his head, a wry smile on his face. 'Stop trying to change the subject. Where were you born? Answer me!'

Gaggenow made an 'oh well, if I must' kind of face and said, 'Umm…the… It was…errr…the North Pole! Yes, of course it was. The North Pole.'

Harry raised a disbelieving eyebrow.

'What?' said Gaggenow. 'I was. I was born at the North Pole.'

'Riiight. Nobody gets born at the North Pole. Come on!' said Harry.

Gaggenow assumed an expression of haughty disdain, and said sniffily, 'Well, I was, so there!'

'Yeah, sure. And what do you do back home, then? You got a job?'

Gaggenow's eyes flicked from side to side shiftily. 'Ummm…'

'What's a'

'job?' whispered the twins.

'If he's from Earth, he'd know,' Harry whispered back. 'Well?' continued Harry, addressing Gaggenow loudly. 'Everyone from Earth has something they do for a living!'

Gaggenow's eyes flicked down to the plastic cup in Harry's hand. 'I…I fix those.'

Harry help up the cup, his face beginning to break into a broad, disbelieving grin.

'I'm a plastic water cup mechanic,' Gaggenow continued, warming to his theme. 'Yes, I fix them when they break,' he said.

Harry began to laugh. 'What a whopper that is!' he said.

'How dare you?' snapped Gaggenow with an arrogant sneer. 'Don't you know who I am?'

'Oh yeah, I do,' said Harry, laughing even more. 'A big fat lying liar is what you are!'

'Nonsense! I am Gaggenow the Magnificent, intergalactic adventurer, explorer of worlds, slayer of miscreants, space pirates and Void Vandals, and the greatest…'

Harry interrupted him. 'Wait a minute, I thought you were a plastic water cup mechanic from Earth!'

Gaggenow blinked. 'Well, yes, that too, the greatest plastic water cup mechanic that ever lived, in fact!'

'You're lying, aren't you?' said Harry.

Gaggenow blinked again, weighing things up for a second or two. Then his shoulders slumped. 'Yes. Yes, I am. Sorry,' he said pitifully.

'Who are you really?' said Alph.

'Just a passenger,' said Gaggenow.

'A stowaway, more like,' said Bet.

'No, I booked a cabin and everything,' spluttered Gaggenow.

'Why didn't the Greys'

'say anything about you, then?' said Alph and Bet.

'Umm…it was a secret! Secret cabin and that. Anonymous passenger…type thing. Because I am so famous. You know, like a VIP.'

The blue-skinned twins rolled their golden eyes in disbelief and made that scornful Yureshtian laughing sound again, a bit like a strangled cat.

'What?' said Gaggenow, his face the picture of unjustly accused innocence. 'It's true!'

'I bet it was you that smashed up that food dispenser, wasn't it?' said Harry.

Gaggenow shifted from foot to foot uncomfortably. 'No, no, that was destroyed in the Leptira attack,' he said.

'Hah, right! Just that and nothing else? A likely story.'

Gaggenow stamped an improbably large foot. 'All right, all right, it was me, but I was hungry, so hungry!'

'So are we,'

'we're hungry too'

'and you ate it all!' said the twins.

'Well, I hadn't eaten for days! Days, I tell you!' said a guilty-looking Gaggenow.

'Why was that, then, if you're a passenger with a cabin and everything? The Greys would have fed you, wouldn't they?' said Harry.

'Not necessarily,' huffed the red-coated Gaggenow.

'Stowaway!'

'We knew it,' said Alph and Bet.

'No, no—'

'Enough of this,' interrupted Harry. 'Where did get your food before all this? You can't have been living off those snack bars all the time.'

'From the ship's galley, of course,' said Gaggenow.

'What, you crept in there and stole stuff?' said Harry.

'Well, I wouldn't say stole as such, I prefer to think of it as…' spluttered Gaggenow, before catching himself and saying, 'No, no, I mean, they brought me food. From the galley. To my cabin. To the Great Gaggenow, as was my due. Of course.'

Gaggenow straightened his bright yellow tie and coughed lightly. Harry turned to Alph and Bet, frowning. 'How come you didn't know about this galley, then?

'Us? Oh no,'

'we're far too high class'

'to get involved with'

'that kind of thing,' said the twins.

'Indeed, they are royal Yureshtian Tsarevnas and should be given the deference pursuant to their station,' said Gaggenow, bowing graciously.

The girls inclined their heads politely and smiled, clearly pleased.

Harry raised an eyebrow. 'Clones of Yureshtian whatsits, that is,' he said brusquely, drawing a 'tsk' and a 'how rude' from the girls.

'Yes, quite! How rude. How boorish! Just what one would expect from a primitive earthman, wouldn't you say, your ladyships?' said Gaggenow.

'You don't know'

'the half of it,' said Alph and Bet.

'What, an earthman just like you, you mean?' said Harry pointedly.

'Me? Oh my, no, I'm a…oh, wait… I mean, yes… errr…' spluttered Gaggenow, his voice trailing off.

'Leave him alone, Harry!'

'He's obviously a better'

'class of human'

'than the average,' said the twins.

'Oh, come on, can't you see he's just saying all that stuff to butter you up?' said Harry.

'Not at all, I'm just a little more cultured, a little better travelled than your ordinary earthling, that's all! And I know how to carry myself in polite society, which is something you should consider learning, young human!' said Gaggenow pompously.

'Yes, something you should'

'consider learning,' echoed the twins, nodding vigorously, like some kind of synchronised nodding team.

Harry didn't like the way things were going. 'Yeah, whatever,' he said. 'Anyway, we all need food, so if you know where this galley is why don't you take us there?'

'Ah, well, that's the problem, you see,' said Gaggenow. 'The Food Replicators in the galley have ceased to function. I suspect the circuitry was in some way disrupted or defibrillated in the Leptira attack, or perhaps some kind of computer security protocol has shut them down. Anyway, now they refuse to work!'

'Any more of those snack machines on board?' said Harry.

'I'm afraid not, that was the only one.' said Gaggenow.

'I knew it,' said Alph. 'We're all going to die.'

'Slowly,' finished Bet.

6 REBOOT

'I can fix it, can I? Cos I'm a boy? Is that it?' said Harry in an astonished voice.

'Not because'

'of that. But because you're'

'a commoner,' said the twin girls, inner eyelids blinking rapidly.

Were they serious or were they taking the mickey? Harry couldn't be sure. Gaggenow, Harry and the blue-skinned twins, Alph and Bet, were standing on the bridge, facing the main computer console.

'To be fair to the untutored descendant of apes, your ladyships, commoner though he obviously is, even a fully grown-up human scientist couldn't fix this computer,' said Gaggenow. 'It is a Flabbergast 9-1000, perhaps one of the best Artificial Intelligences ever built by the Greys, and they know how to construct AIs, oh yes, by my ageratch wikwak foodle butt, they do!'

Harry's brow furrowed. He tapped the translator in his ear. It crackled back with 'ageratch wikwak foodle butt – dizzy father's sister,' then crackled again and ended finally with 'my giddy aunt'.

It was an old expression that hardly anyone used any more but still, he had to admit, the translator knew its stuff.

'Let me try again – Computer! Activate food replicators. Dinner for four – nutritional requirements: two Yureshtian, one Earth human and one…errrr…no, sorry, correction – two Earth humans, of course!' said Gaggenow.

There was a pause and then a robotic voice said, 'Minimal Operational Functionality. Unable to activate Food Replication Service. Please take your Flabbergast 9-1000 to your nearest Quantum Digital Ltd Service Station.'

'Surely you can fix it, Earth boy. I mean, you are so common!' said Alph.

'No!' said Harry, shrugging.

'You could at least take a look…' said Bet.

Harry rolled his eyes. 'All right, I'll take a look, just to keep you happy.'

He stepped up to the main computer console. A bank of lights and readouts flickered confusingly. He tried to find something that made sense, but there wasn't really any similarity with the computers he was used to back home.

'Where's the keyboard?' he muttered to himself.

'Keyboard On,' said the computer, and suddenly a keyboard appeared out of thin air, causing Harry to step back in surprise. A keyboard made of light. Solid light. It had actual keys, though, even if they

were holographic and covered in strange symbols, tightly packed in a circular configuration. No doubt designed for the Greys and their little squid-like, multi-jointed tentacle 'fingers'. Harry tried pushing a key or two, and immediately a screen display popped into the air in front of him. A message appeared in an alien script. It began to flash.

'What does that say?' said Harry.

The girls shrugged. 'We don't read Grey,' they said in unison. Gaggenow shook his head.

'Computer, use standard…errr…human. Human Earth English!' said Harry.

The letters on the screen duly morphed into English. 'Warning: Keyboard Malfunction' it read.

Now it was Harry's turn to shrug. 'Nothing I can do,' he said.

'We're going to starve to death,'

'just as I thought,' said the twins.

The four of them stared glumly at the computer: Gaggenow with his head slightly bowed, his hands dangling listlessly at his sides; the twins staring at each other's feet; and Harry with his arms folded, brow furrowed in thought. But then Harry noticed something, something he almost recognised, amidst all the buttons, lights, readouts, dials and indicators. It looked like this:

He reached forward and pushed it. Suddenly, all the lights went out, everywhere.

'OMG!' said Bet, (or so the translator said; what she actually said was something like 'Ay Ay, Bahmin Fahmin Boodle!')

'What have you done, Earth boy?' said Alph.

Harry swallowed nervously. What had he done? The lights didn't come back on, and after a few seconds the temperature began to drop.

'Oh my,' said Gaggenow, 'I think you turned off the life support! We'll be dead in minutes!'

'Well, better'n starving to death, right?' said Harry, desperately searching the console for a solution.

'No, no, I can't die!' wailed Gaggenow. 'Not I, not poor Gaggenow, poor poor Gaggenow, the greatest artist that ever lived! To die here alone in space like this, it can't be…'

'Alone? What about us,'

'don't we count?' said the twins.

'You? Of course you don't…' Just then, the console began to flicker back to life, and the lights came on. Gaggenow's expression changed from a sneer to an ingratiating smile. '…don't deserve to die like this either, my ladyships, and I just want to say what an honour it is to die alongside two such lovely noble Tsarevnas as yourselves!'

The twins looked up at him, heads tilted to one side, and beamed.

'How polite'

'how courteous!' they said, as they turned to look at Harry pointedly.

Harry shook his head in disgust. Then the temperature began to rise and a monitor popped into place out of nowhere. Numbers and letters began to stream across the screen and a computer voice began to warble at them in Grey. The translator kicked in.

'Initialising…

'Detecting Factory Settings…

'Flabbergast 9-1000…

'Installing Operating System…

'Hardware: Deep Recon Wheelship Model Type AG85CLE-FW569…

'Canus Prime Shipyard, Hub licence: 58934935278430505.'

'Oh my, could it be that we are not going to perish, alone here in the cold, dark depths of space after all?' said Gaggenow, observing the twins out of the corner of his eye.

'I knew you'

'were common enough'

'to fix it, Earth boy!' they said, clapping their hands together with glee.

'No, I just pushed—' But before Harry could finish, the computer interrupted him.

'User Name?' it said.

'Errr, Harry,' said Harry.

'Captain Harry. Welcome aboard the Deep Recon Wheelship Model Type AG85CLE-FW569.'

'Captain? I'm not a captain!'

'Yeah,'

'no way!' said the twins.

'Captain Harry,' said the computer. 'What are your instructions?'

Before Harry could say a word, Gaggenow stepped forward, 'Computer, do not listen to this ignorant Earth boy. The true captain is I, Captain Gaggenow!'

'What!' said Harry. 'Leave it out, you creep,' he added, reaching over to give Gaggenow a push, but before he could the computer spoke again. 'Captain Gaggenow not recognised.'

Harry grinned a 'So there' grin, but Gaggenow wasn't going to give up so easily. 'Bah!' he said. 'Did I say Captain Gaggenow? I meant Admiral Gaggenow, of course! Computer! These are your instructions. You will cease to pay any attention to this primitive earthling, but listen only to me, Admiral Gaggenow! And you will address me as Admiral Gaggenow the Magnificent!'

'Admiral Gaggenow not recognised. Captain Harry, instructions, please,' said the computer.

'Hah!' said Harry triumphantly. 'So there! I'm still the captain!'

'Bah, just because you turned it on, how absurd!' said Gaggenow.

'Eat it, alien freak!' said Harry.

'Hey, I'm as human as you are,' retorted Gaggenow.

'Riiiight!' said Harry.

'Excuse us, but we are'

'starving here, and we'

'really would like to eat'

'it too,' said the twins.

'Heh, I'd like you to eat it as well, but yes, of course!' said Harry with a grin. 'Computer?'

'Yes, Captain?'

'Can you activate the food replicators?'

'Yes, Captain, replicators activated.' The computer paused and then went on, 'Replicators functioning at fifty per cent capacity. Widespread damage affecting most ship systems.'

'But they can make food?'

'Affirmative, but Nutrit only,' said the computer. The twins sighed. Gaggenow actually groaned.

'What's Nutrit?' said Harry.

'All bio-unit nutritional requirements packed into an easily digestible food paste,' said the computer.

'Tastes revolting,' said Gaggenow.

'Nutrit Porridge now available in Ship Galley,' said the computer. The four of them looked at each other. It might be some kind of hideous alien porridge but no one had eaten for hours and hours and they were all ravenous.

'This way!' said Gaggenow, and they all ran for the galley as fast as they could.

7 UNMASKED

FOUR figures stood at the Observation Dome's Gallery, gazing out into deep space. Everywhere was blackness, a yawning abyss of nothing…except for a hand-sized patch of light off in the far, far distance. The galaxy.

Harry felt a moment of head-spinning dizziness. It all seemed totally unreal. How could he be here? It must be a dream, right? He'd wake up at any moment, find himself in bed back home, his mum bringing him a cup of tea as she woke him up for school. He'd set off, hoping not to have a run-in with Scars and his gang. And after school, maybe he'd go and see his mate Harvey, and…

A long whistling sound disturbed his train of thought. He looked over – it was Gaggenow. Then the twins also sighed.

Harry shook his head. Nope, it was real, all of

it. Here he was on a spaceship on the wrong side of the galaxy, standing next to three weirdo aliens. Incredible, but real.

The alien trio sighed again.

'What is it with all the sighing?' said Harry. 'I've instructed the computer to set a course back to our galaxy. What more can we do?'

Gaggenow and the twins exchanged looks. Gaggenow mouthed something at the twins, but Harry couldn't make it out – the translator couldn't lip-read, after all.

'It's not his fault he's'

'stupid, he's only human,' said the girls.

'Hey, right here!' said Harry indignantly.

'You see, ignorant earthling,' said Gaggenow, 'the ship is out of hyper fuel. Because you used it all up.'

'Used it up! Saved the ship and all of us from certain death at the hands of the Leptira, more like!' said Harry.

'The Leptira'

'don't have hands,'

'they have,'

'errr'

'…thingies,' added the girls.

'Indeed. But my point is that Harry here failed to turn off the Quantum Drive, condemning us all to death anyway,' said Gaggenow.

'Oh, I see, so I should have let us all die at the "thingies" of the Leptira, is that it?' said Harry.

'You might as well have! You see, Harry—'

'That's Captain Harry to you!' interjected Harry.

'You see, HARRY,' continued Gaggenow in a pompous, lecturing tone, 'all we have left as a power source are the Fusion Banks. Powerful enough, to be sure, but designed for Intrasolar travel. They're nothing compared to hyper speeds. We're already hurtling away from the galaxy at a prodigious velocity – it is going to take us weeks just to bring the ship to a halt. And then…well…' Gaggenow's voice trailed off in despair.

'Well what? We can survive for a few months, easy!' said Harry.

'Yes, indeed, but with what Fusion fuel we have remaining, it will take us about a hundred years or more to get back to our galaxy.'

'Ah… I see…' said Harry, racking his brains. It sounded bad, very bad, but he wouldn't give up. There had to be something they could do!

Gaggenow smiled a paternal smile down at Harry and the twins. 'Perhaps it is time you children gave over command of things to me. I'm the only one who really knows what's going on, after all!'

'Seems'

'reasonable,' said the twins.

'No way!' said Harry. 'I'll think of something – how far away is it, anyway?'

'Oh, millions'

'and millions'

'and millions'

'of light years,' said the girls.

'What we can see, the light from our galaxy, is coming to us from millions and millions of years in the past,' said Gaggenow wistfully. He glanced at Harry. 'Somewhere in there is Earth, millions of years old.'

The twins looked at each other, blinking their weird blink, and smiled.

'Your ancestors are rubbing sticks together to make fire.'

'Or swinging through the trees.'

'Or grubbing about in a swamp.'

'Or—'

'Yeah, I get it,' said Harry.

'So,' said Gaggenow, 'I shall be assuming command then, yes?'

The twins nodded. Harry shook his head angrily. 'Hold on, who are you, anyway?'

'The Great Gaggenow, obviously,' said Gaggenow, straightening his shoulders and assuming a regal bearing.

'Yeah, right, but who is Gaggenow really? Computer, what have you got on file for a

"Gaggenow"? A "Ribshack Gaggenow"!' said Harry.

A holographic monitor appeared in the air. Gaggenow frowned. The monitor flashed to life, and a curious fish-like face appeared with a stream of writing in Grey characters below it.

'Computer, translate,' said Harry.

'Wanted, Dead or Alive!' began the computer. 'For crimes against the Imperium, including Theft, Blackmail, Corrupting a Galactic Official, Fraud, Intrinsic Fraud, Extrinsic Fraud, Collateral Fraud, Constructive Fraud, Fraud in the Factum, Fraud in the Inducement, etc, etc, the Ichthysupial Rib Nib Dib, alias Gaggenow, Gaggenow the Magnificent, the Great Gaggenow. Bounty: one million Galactic Credits, dead or alive (preferably dead). Also, any other beings found with him should be deemed to be his accomplices and dealt with accordingly. By order of GalPol, Hub Prime.'

Harry's jaw dropped in astonishment. The twins' eyes widened into golden discs.

'GalPol?' said Harry.

'Galactic'

'Police.'

'Right! I bet that's why the Leptira attacked us, for the reward!' said Harry.

'They are known to dabble in'

'bounty hunting, it is true,' said the twins.

Harry turned on Gaggenow, eyes blazing. Gaggenow took a step back, his eyes shifting from side to side, looking as guilty as a villain in a pantomime.

'So it's all your fault!' shouted Harry.

'No, no, it's a mistake! I mean, look! I don't look anything like that picture, do I?' protested Gaggenow.

'That's true,'

'you don't!' said Alph and Bet.

'Well, OK,' said Harry, 'but there's still something fishy going on. You're obviously not human. And you call yourself Gaggenow. The Great Gaggenow, even! And you said your name was Rib at first, before changing it to Ribshack, which all fits!'

'That's true too!' said the twins together.

'Come on, then, tell us the truth, once and for all,' shouted Harry, stepping right up to Gaggenow and prodding him in the chest with a finger.

Suddenly, there was a flash of light and Gaggenow fell backwards to the floor with a cry. He landed in a flurry of gangling limbs with more than the regulation one elbow or knee apiece, no longer looking human at all, but something…well, something completely different.

'A hologram harness!' said Alph, sounding as outraged as if she'd caught someone cheating in an exam.

Gaggenow didn't have a red suit on, or a yellow tie, and he wasn't grey or blue, but rather a maggoty white colour. Stunned by being tipped onto his backside, he gazed up with eyes that looked far too narrow and close-set to be trustworthy, whatever solar system you came from. He had a long, startled-looking face that reminded Harry of a goldfish. The lower part of his body looked a bit like an incredibly wiry kangaroo, with enormous floppy feet. The harness Alph had referred to was a contraption like a tangle of seat belts that wound around a brownish tunic on his thin and bony torso. There was a panel with buttons on the front, and Harry twigged that his finger had shut the device off.

'You've been lying to us all along!' said Harry. Gaggenow drew something from a pocket in his tunic and pointed it at them. The two girls drew away with a gasp. Harry looked down. There was a wide patch of light moving across his chest.

Gaggenow clambered to his feet. 'Don't make a move or I shoot,' he said, darting a nervous glance towards the door.

'Let him go,' said Bet.

'He sounds like he means business,' agreed Alph.

'That's my *phone*,' said Harry.

'Eh?' Gaggenow's mouth gaped, making the resemblance to a goldfish even more noticeable.

'That gun you're holding,' said Harry. 'It's not a gun. It's my phone – you thief. I bet you had it out of my pocket while I was laid out in the control room, eh?'

'Don't antagonise him!' said Bet.

'I warn you, stand back,' said the tall alien. 'Don't trifle with the Great Gaggenow. Look, I'm setting my blaster to lethal intensity.'

He fiddled with the phone. It played the ringtone – a few bars of the *Astropocalypse* game theme. Gaggenow stabbed at another button and the light switched off.

Harry snatched it out of his hand. 'You're the most rubbish evil alien I've met all day.'

'Er…it's a grenade, not a gun after all,' said Gaggenow. 'You'd better run away or it will blow up and kill you all.'

'Quick, throw it into the airlock!' screamed Bet.

'Get a grip! It's my phone that this creep took off me while I was unconscious.'

'I…found it,' said Gaggenow defensively.

'Where? Where did you find it?'

'It was…near…um…'

'Because I keep it in this pocket, which as you can see has a button-down flap. So don't tell me it fell out.'

'I was trying to revive you,' countered Gaggenow.

'Oh, ta. And yet somehow you wandered off with my phone instead?'

'I thought...I thought it was a weapon! I'm sorry, I was scared, really scared. The Leptira – you know, the LEPTIRA! They were after me, and in one of their battle cruisers as well. I was terrified!' With that he put his big, bony, four-fingered hands up to his goldfish-like head and sobbed.

Harry sighed. 'You...you should have told us earlier instead of lying to us,' he said. Yes, Gaggenow was a hopeless liar and a cheat, and he looked like a freaky alien, but he was all skin and bone, and kind of vulnerable-looking.

'And then what? Have you hand me over for the reward? If the Greys had found me, they would have handed me over without a thought. Why would you be any different?'

'So, you *were*'

'a stowaway, after all!' said the twins.

'Well, duh! Of course he was,' said Harry. 'He's just hiding from the police!'

Suddenly a klaxon sounded – a bit like the red alert sound on the *Enterprise* in *Star Trek*, actually.

'Warning! Warning! An object has been detected heading towards us.'

'A…a what?' said Harry?

'An unidentified object. Telemetry and Sensors are only functioning at twenty-seven per cent. Unable to determine nature of object yet. Object is travelling at near hyper speed and is approaching fast.'

Gaggenow got to his big, floppy kangaroo feet. 'Out here in the deep gulfs of space? How is that possible?' he said. 'Unless it's…'

'What? Unless it's what?'

'Void Vandals,' said Gaggenow in a quavering voice.

'Void Vandals? What are Void Vandals?'

'Criminals that'

'use the Void'

'to hide in'

'and to raid the galaxy,' said Alph and Bet.

'Oh, like pirates, you mean?'

'Precisely,' said Gaggenow. 'Ruthless, murdering, brutal pirates.'

'Oh, great, this is just getting better and better! Where is this object, Computer?' said Harry.

'Over there,' said the computer. A holographic hand, shaped like the hand of a Grey, appeared in the air, and pointed a squid-like jointed tentacle to a bright light in the black emptiness. It had a long, long tail of matter behind it, like a bluish-white vapour trail.

'Looks like a comet,' said Alph.

'Yes, indeed,' said Gaggenow. 'It does, thankfully!'

'So, not Void Vandals, then?' said Harry, almost disappointed.

'No, they have'

'big spaceships'

'with lots of guns,' said the twins.

Gaggenow frowned. 'Still, something isn't right. That vapour trail…strange, out here so far from any suns…and what are the odds we'd find a comet so near to us?'

'Perhaps it's just a big'

'cosmic coincidence,' said the twins.

'Perhaps…' said Gaggenow.

'Nucleus of object appears to be composed of frozen water, gases and interstellar dust,' said the computer. 'Object appears to be a comet.'

'Well, there you are,' said Bet.

'Computer, how close will the comet get to us?' said Harry.

'Current trajectory will take it very close to our ship,' said the computer. 'If there is a collision, this ship will be vaporised immediately. Shields are operating at three per cent.'

'Extraordinary!' said Gaggenow. 'The odds of that happening by chance must be truly astronomical!'

'Shall I take evasive action, Captain?' said the computer.

Harry stared at the approaching comet, brow furrowed in thought, trying to think of a way of getting out of this. And not just that. Of using it to their advantage. But how?

8 · NO COMET

THE comet was hurtling towards them. Gaggenow and the twins stood at the Observation Dome gallery, staring impotently up at it.

'Comet has an anomalous gravitational reading. Mass is heavier than it should be if composed entirely of frozen water, interstellar gas and dust,' said the computer.

Harry was thinking about *Astropocalypse*. Best game ever. But what was that new tech he'd discovered...? Some kind of energy beam thing for picking up stuff – Tractor Beams, that was it!

'Computer, does this ship have a tractor beam?'

'A...what?' said the twins.

'You know, tractor beam thingy whatsit,' said Harry.

'Tractor Beam not recognised; please clarify,' said the computer.

'An energy beam that grips things, like a crane or a grab or something. But made of…umm…well, energy.' His voice tailed off at the end as he realised how unlikely it sounded.

'Ah, you mean a device like the Gravitronic Grapple!' said Gaggenow. 'Yes, of course, all ships have those for docking. The Greys' Grapple is particularly strong, as they use it for harvesting people and materials, like the grubbing little scavengers that they are.'

'Cool,' said Harry. 'Computer, calculate exact… errr…what is it, you know, the path of the comet…'

'Trajectory?' said Gaggenow.

'Yeah, that's it! Computer, calculate current trajectory of the comet and display on screen.'

'Yes, Captain,' said the computer.

The holographic monitor flashed an image of the comet sweeping past their ship, then arcing off and heading straight for the galaxy at enormous speed. In doing so, it would bathe their ship in its vapour trail.

'Perfect!' said Harry.

'What? Why? Who knows what's in that vapour

trail; it could be superheated plasma or something!' said Gaggenow.

'That doesn't'

'sound good!' said Alph and Bet.

'Absolutely – the ship would melt in seconds, and so would we,' said Gaggenow. 'We have to take evasive action!'

'No, no, this is our only chance,' said Harry. The comet drew closer at a furious speed, looking for all the world like it was going to slam right into them.

'We should get'

'out of the way!' shrieked the girls.

'Computer, take evasive action immediately, and that's an order!' shouted Gaggenow.

'No, don't! Stay where we are,' said Harry forcefully.

'Are you mad, foolish earthling?' said Gaggenow.

'Trust me, I've got a plan,' said Harry.

'Really? The adolescent stripling from Earth has a plan? Ridiculous. COMPUTER, TAKE EVASIVE ACTION, NOW!'

'Yes, now, now!' echoed the twins.

'Captain Harry, confirm Evasive Action order,' said the computer.

'No, don't do it! Keep the ship where it is,' said Harry. 'If we die now – so what? We're going to die anyway, right, stuck out here in empty space!'

'Yes, but possibly of old age instead of vaporised in a fiery inferno! There's a difference, you know,' said Gaggenow.

'Except that you said the fuel would run out – when that goes, what powers the ships then? Life support will die, and so will we,' quipped Harry.

'Now you are'

'splitting hairs,' said the twins.

Gaggenow began to drum his huge floppy kangaroo feet on the floor in panic. He put his bony, four-fingered, four-knuckled hands over his head and said, 'I don't want to die! I'm begging you, CAPTAIN Harry, tell the computer to change course, please!'

'No, I'm not giving up,' said Harry.

Gaggenow stared at him in disbelief. The twins' eyes were wide saucers of gold. The comet drew closer.

And closer.

And closer still, getting larger and larger all the time.

They all craned their necks, looking up as it began to fill the observation window, an enormous ball of fizzing blue-white energy, and then suddenly they were within its corona, its field of dust and light. They could see the surface of the comet itself, a dirty, ice-covered ball of rock.

'AIIIIEEEEE...'

'...EEEEEEEEE!!!!' howled Gaggenow and the twins.

'Computer, prepare to activate Gravi— errr. Grapple thing,' said Harry.

'Gravitronic Grapple?' queried the computer. 'To grapple the comet?'

'Yeah, that's it, get it ready…wait for it, wait for it…'

Then the comet began to curve away. The trail of bright blue vapour, or whatever it was, began to come round. It touched the hull of the ship…

Gaggenow was peeking through the many knuckles of his hands. The twins' eyes were wider than Harry had ever seen, like great golden suns. Actually quite beautiful, really, but he wasn't going to tell them that.

The Observation Dome was bathed in a bright bluish-white light and…

…and…

…and they weren't vaporised or melted or burnt, they didn't explode or shatter, shrivel or disintegrate.

Harry laughed out loud in relief, but then his laughter faded to puzzlement. The bluish-white light began to play up and down their bodies and around the interior of the ship, covering everything with light. The twins held up their hands and looked at them as they glowed white and blue, like ghosts.

'It's almost as if it were searching for something,' said Gaggenow.

'Well, whatever,' said Harry. 'The important thing is that we're still alive!'

The comet began to accelerate away. 'Computer, now! Do the grapple thing!' shouted Harry.

A ray of brown light, inlaid with streams of greenish energy, flicked out from their ship and attached itself to the comet. They all lurched forward with the impact, as the ship accelerated to the same speed as the comet.

Harry folded his arms and grinned triumphantly. 'See,' he said, 'we're still alive. And heading back to the galaxy; how cool is that?'

'Bah, luck!' said Gaggenow, getting to his feet. 'Just blind luck!'

'Luck? Brilliant plan, more like!' said Harry.

'Estimated time of arrival at Galactic Fringe at present velocity: four days,' said the computer.

'There! How about that, then?' said Harry. 'Brilliant or what?'

The twins exchanged a look and then turned to Harry.

'Well'

'done,' they said in an almost-whisper.

'What? What was that?' said Harry, leaning forward and grinning an even bigger grin. 'Did you say what I thought you said?'

They looked at each other. And nodded. Ever so slightly.

'"Well done", eh!' said Harry. 'I thought so. How about thanking me too? You know, for saving your life and that!'

The twins stared at him.

'Don't'

'push it, Earth boy!' they hissed.

Harry laughed. He was enjoying this, really enjoying it. It was like breaking up for the school holidays, but ten times better.

Then the bluish-white tail of the comet winked out of existence. Just like that. So did the smile on Harry's face. What was happening now?

Suddenly, something moved on the surface of the comet. Something small and round. It looked like a hatch or a door, opening. And out of it something… oozed.

Gaggenow, Harry and the twins stared in fascination, jaws agape. What the…?

The oozing thing grew into a fat blob of brownish sludge, a bit like a perfectly round blob of mud. The blob extruded a thin stalk straight upwards. The end of the stalk formed itself into a flat, wide disc which suddenly winked open to reveal a huge eye! An eye that stared at them, unblinkingly.

They stared back, astounded. Then it began to extrude a tentacle from its side. The tentacle reached down into the open hatchway and came back out, holding what appeared to be a small black rectangular device. Its eye bent down to examine the device. Another tentacle appeared, and began to press what were presumably buttons or switches. Then it held the device up to the side of its body and its eye came back up to examine them.

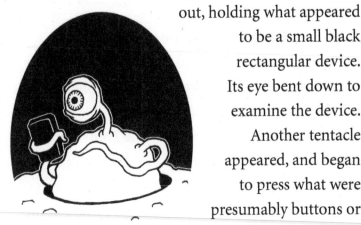

Suddenly Harry's phone began to play the *Astropocalypse* ringtone.

'Whoa!' Harry jumped. Surely it wasn't…it couldn't…could it?

'Answer it,' hissed Gaggenow.

'No way!' said Harry. 'I'm not talking to that… that brown thing!'

'Go on,'

'answer it,'

'you idiot,' said the girls, gesturing at him in unison.

The brown round blob jabbed a tentacle at Harry, and then at the device it was holding, as if to say, 'Answer your phone, cretin!'

Harry reached for his phone. Gingerly he picked it up and looked at the screen.

'Caller Unknown,' it said. That was for sure! He hit the answer button and put it up to his ear.

'Fleeplub weechle meechle, bleechle bleeble weeble peeble,' oozed a voice in his ear, all blubbery mud and suppurating slime, like the sound of a swamp.

The translator device in his ear said, 'Language unknown. Unable to translate.'

Harry held the phone up, and pointed at it,

shrugging and shaking his head. The brown blob waved a tentacle and pointed back at Harry's phone. Harry placed it to his ear again. This time the translator understood.

'Sorry, sorry, I'm using PanGal now,' said the brown blob.

'PanGal?' said Harry, confused.

'Yeah, you know, PanGalactic.'

'PanGalactic?' said Harry, still not getting it.

'Yeah, PanGalactic, the common language of the galaxy, PanGal. How can you not…ah, I get it, you're not from round here, are you?'

'No, no, I'm not,' said Harry. 'I'm from Earth.'

'Earth? Never heard of it,' warbled the blob.

'How did you get this number?' said Harry unthinkingly.

'Well, as you've probably realised, this isn't a comet at all, but an Inscrutable Ballistic Orb,' began the creature.

'Ah…what?' said Harry.

'An Inscrutable…umm…a spaceship in disguise, I suppose you'd call it,' said the tentacled blob.

'Spaceship in the skies?' said Harry, still not really

believing what was going on, and a bit slow because of it.

'No, IN DISGUISE, idiot! Anyway, the vapour trail is in fact Sssh-An's Stupefyingly Sagacious Decrypticon,' said the brown blob.

'Sssh…Stupe…what?'

'Stupefying Decrypticon – you know, a…umm…a kind of sensor beam, I guess.'

'Ahhh…' said Harry.

'We've analysed your ship and everything in it, including that primitive communication device of yours. Easy peasy to get the codes with the Decrypticon.'

'Oh,' said Harry.

'What's'

'going on?' said the twins.

'Tell us what the creature is saying,' said Gaggenow.

'Right,' said Harry. 'Hold on,' he said to the brown thing, 'I'm putting you on speakerphone.'

'Fine by me,' it said.

'OK, go ahead,' said Harry.

'Anyway,' said the tentacled blob, its strange warbling, squelching voice echoing tinnily out of

Harry's phone (the twins and Gaggenow were fluent in PanGal, of course), 'you seem to have locked onto us with a—'

'But what the hell *are* you?' interrupted Harry.

'Me? A Coagulite. That's what they call us, Coagulites. From Glob.'

'Glob?'

'Yeah, the planet Glob.'

A blob from Glob! *Riiight*, thought Harry to himself.

'Have you got a name?' he said.

'Of course, I'm Awesomely Equanimous Plenipotentiary Dee-Ung, of the Globular Consulate.'

'Wha…what was that again?'

'You're not very bright, are you? Let me see, how to make it simple? Err…Ambassador, I guess. Ambassador of Cool. You can call me Ambassador Dee-Ung.'

'Ambassador Dung!!!! You've got to be kidding me!'

'No! Dee-Ung. There's a difference, you know.'

Harry put his hand over his mouth, trying not to laugh.

'Anyway,' said Dee-Ung, 'we detected you out here in the Intergalactic Void, and decided to investigate. Which we did. And found you to be of little interest, unusual though it is to find your various species out here. But then you locked onto us with your Gravitronic Grapple. This is unacceptable.'

'Why? We're just hitching a lift,' said Harry.

'Hitching a... Listen, Meatstick, we—'

But before he could finish, Harry interrupted him again. 'Meatstick, what's that supposed to mean?' he said.

'Eh? Oh, that. That's just what we call life forms with their flesh and organs and that hung on a skeletal structure. Meat-on-a-stick. Meatstick. I mean, all those bones, and organs and things – talk about weird!!!'

'Oh, right, I get it,' said Harry. 'But I have a name too. It's Harry.'

'Well, all right, then. Now, listen to me, Harry, you can't just hitch a lift whenever you like – for a start, your ship is draining our Zest, not to mention the effect it's having on our Really Clever Empennageral Stabilisers!'

'I'll remove the Grapple as soon as we reach the galaxy,' said Harry. 'I promise!'

'Unacceptable! All Zest will be Defunctuated by then! Decouple your ship now, or we will be forced to Irrupt the Decrypticon with Zest until it becomes a De-Yleminator!'

'Ylem what?'

'Umm…blast you out of space with our Death Ray, type thing.'

'You wouldn't'

'dare!'

'We're royalty,'

'you know!' said the twins.

'Oh yes, I would,' said Ambassador Dee-Ung. 'And anyway, you're clones of royalty, and out here, who'd know?'

'Oh, how rude.'

'It's just not done'

'to mention such things,' said the twins.

'Yeah, well, whatever,' said the ambassador. 'The fact is, you've got to Decouple your ship immediately, or face the consequences. And remember, we know your shields are minimal and your weapons array disabled.'

'Of course, your Excellency, we will do as you ask straight away, there's no need for the De-Yleminator!' said Gaggenow. And he turned to Harry, gesticulating vigorously with his four-knuckled fingers, as his floppy kangaroo feet drummed the ground in fear.

Harry scowled. He didn't like being threatened. 'Hold on, if we let go of you, we're doomed anyway, as we'll just drift aimlessly through the…what did you call it? The Void. And then die out here, all alone. Be better for us if you did put us out of our misery right now, so go ahead, do it!'

'Noooooo…' said Gaggenow and the twins in unison.

9 UNDER MY SKIN

'DON'T listen to him, your Most Esteemed and Merciful Supremely Magnificent Excellency!' said Gaggenow. 'He's just a primitive Earth boy – their planet hasn't even been tagged for pre-space monitoring; they haven't even discovered fusion – in fact, his species hasn't even left their own planet yet!'

'Yes, we have,' said Harry. 'We went to the moon and everything!'

'Oh, pleeaase! Might as well be the next room as far as real spacefaring is concerned.'

'Interesting,' said Dee-Ung. 'He may be a piece of meat that's barely crawled out of the back end of evolution, but he's got guts, and he does appear to be in charge. The Ship's Computer confirms it too.'

'Bah, absurd. Ridiculous! Computer error – a glitch, a bug, has to be,' said Gaggenow angrily. 'I should be in charge!'

'Computer error? Really? I mean, it's one of those famous Flabbergast constructs, isn't it, supposed to be the best computers in the galaxy! Error? I don't think so!' said the brown, round, blob-like ambassador.

'Well, it's true,' said Harry. 'I'm the captain, and I'm not turning the grapple off and that's that.'

The ambassador's single eye blinked. Gaggenow fumed. Harry folded his arms. Alph and Bet stared, golden-eyed.

Then Alph said, 'Hold on, you're heading to the galaxy anyway. So if we let go we'd continue on the same course,' and Bet finished, 'at the same speed, and get there anyway?'

'Yes, indeed!' said the ambassador. 'And we won't have to reduce your atoms to nothingness after all!'

'Except,' said Harry, 'we'd just end up at some random place at the edge of the galaxy without the means to actually get anywhere where there's people and food and fuel and stuff. Let alone Earth. We'd be in same boat we are in now, just not here, but there.'

Gaggenow nodded. 'Actually, that's true.'

'Well,' said the ambassador, 'we could orientate the Inscrutable Ballistic Orb in such a way that when you let go, your course would be heading straight for a Galactic Fringe outpost of some kind. Bound to be something…hold on, let me have a look.' The Coagulite's eye stalk snaked down through the hatch, extending to an improbable length. Seconds later it returned.

'I've had a gander at our Star Charts – the nearest thing is a Triple V Space Station called the Leaf Star, how about that?'

'Triple V?' said Harry.

'Void Vista Vacation. They're like these luxurious hotels in space that Meatsticks go to, so they can be at the edge of the galaxy and look out on absolutely nothing. Who knows why!'

'That'd be perfect,' said Gaggenow, 'I could do with a holiday! Not to mention it being…well, out of the way.'

'All right, then,' said Dee-Ung, 'but that, of course, would be doing you a favour, as it'll cost us time and Zest. So that would have to be a Deal.'

'A deal?

'Yes, a transaction, a Deal. I mean, what do we get out of it? In effect, we are towing you back home. We should get paid for that.'

'Paid?'

'Yes, PAID! You know, with Galactic Credits or something – come on, get with the programme!' said Ambassador Dee-Ung.

'Umm…I haven't got any Credits. You guys?' said Harry, turning to Gaggenow and the twins.

Gaggenow shrugged, holding out his hands in the universal gesture of 'I ain't got jack'. The twins shook their heads in unison.

'Umm…we haven't got any money,' said Harry.

'Well, in that case, there is another option,' said the round brown thing, silkily. If it was possible for a warbling mound of brown goo to say something silkily.

'What's that, then?' said Harry, suspicious.

'We call it an Indentured Liability,' said the ambassador.

Gaggenow drew in a sharp breath. The twins began to shake their heads vigorously. Harry frowned.

'What?' he said to Gaggenow.

Gaggenow looked down at the back of his hand. 'Oh, nothing,' he said. 'Nothing to worry about.'

Harry looked over at the twins. They turned away and looked up at the ceiling. And began to whistle. The same tune. In perfect harmony.

Harry looked back at the strange brown alien thing that looked like a blob perched on the outside of a disguised comet ship, hurtling through the empty void of nothingness between galaxies, that was talking to him on his mobile phone. And shook his head in disbelief.

'All right, I'll bite,' he said. 'What's an Indentured Liability?'

'Well, basically you will owe us a favour, some time in the future when we need it. Could be any time, but we'll give you fair notice when we're calling it in.'

Harry frowned. It didn't sound that bad. So how come the reaction from Gaggenow and the twins?

'What kind of favour?' said Harry.

'Oh, something similar, it won't be out of proportion or anything. Or fatal, you know...

something reasonable.'

'Well, all right, that sounds OK,' said Harry.

'Of course, we have to make sure you stick to the Deal. And that we can reach you whenever we can, when the time comes.'

'Seems fair enough.' Harry nodded.

'So, I'll send over an Indenturesite. Do you agree?'

'A what? An Indent— a what?'

'Indenturesite. A little bit of me. It'll burrow into your body, and hide inside, out of the way. Like a parasite, but a symbiotic one. It won't do you any harm, just sleep there until the time comes that we need our favour, and it'll wake up and ask you,' said Ambassador Dee-Ung in a rush of words.

Harry just stared in horrified amazement. He turned to Gaggenow, who smiled back reassuringly as if what had just been said was as normal as apple pie.

'It'll be fine,' he said. 'Don't you worry!' Harry turned to the twins – they were now looking down, examining each other's shoes and ignoring him completely.

Harry turned back to the ambassador. Dee-Ung

plucked a little globule of himself, rolled it up between some tentacled fingers like it was a bogey, and said, 'Open up one of your Small Freight Airlock doors, and I'll send this through.'

Harry stared in horror, desperately trying to think of an alternative.

'It's either this, or we De-Yleminate you. Or you drift off on your own and take your chances in the Void. Maybe some Void Vandals will find you… though death would be better'n that,' said Dee-Ung.

'Go on, it'll be fine,' said Gaggenow. 'A little alien worm under the skin. Inside you. What could possibly go wrong?'

'We have'

'no choice,' said Alph and Bet.

'"We"? Me, you mean!' said Harry.

'Captain's responsibility,' said Gaggenow with an evil grin. The twins shrugged in agreement.

119

'Well, I suppose I have to. OK, then. Computer, open a small airlock,' said Harry resignedly.

'Excellent!' said the ambassador. He placed the little piece of himself inside a small container, and let it go. The container fired up tiny rockets and sped off towards the ship, somewhere down below, out of sight of the Observation Deck.

'Alien Cargo Acquired. Warning: Life Signs Detected. Quarantine or Allow on Board? Quarantine recommended,' said the computer.

Harry sighed. 'Allow it on board.'

'Yes, Captain,' said the computer.

'As soon as you've been Indenturesited, we'll programme a course for you,' said the ambassador. 'And don't worry, the procedure is not painful. Well, not really.'

A small black device buzzed into the Observation Dome. It flew straight at Harry, and then hovered in front of him. A little hatch slid open, and out flew a tiny brown worm. It shot forward and landed on Harry's arm. He recoiled in disgust and horror.

'Whoa!' he shouted, raising his other hand as if to swat the little worm instantly.

'Calm down, calm down,' said the ambassador. 'Really, it's not as bad as it looks, trust me.'

Suddenly the brown worm began to burrow its way into Harry's skin. It began to hurt, like a really, really painful spot or a boil.

'No, wait,' shouted Harry. 'I've changed my mind – stop, stop!' he screamed, trying to pull the worm thing out, but he couldn't get any purchase – it seemed to flow around his fingers like water.

'Changed your mind? Unacceptable! You can't

just renegotiate a contract whenever you like, you know,' said the ambassador testily. 'I mean, a Deal's a Deal, right? Surely that's true on your planet just as it is on pretty much every planet in the galaxy?'

The worm slipped in under Harry's skin and the pain stopped.

'Well, yes, I suppose it is,' said Harry as the brown worm disappeared somewhere inside him. It was too late now anyway. And the ambassador did have a point.

'You're a brave lad, for a primitive earthling, I'll give you that,' said Gaggenow.

'Yes, it's true,'

'you are a'

'brave commoner,'

'as you should be'

'in the service of your betters,' said Alph and Bet.

'Yeah, thanks for that, guys, that really makes me feel better,' said Harry wryly. 'Anyway, Ambassador, I've accepted your...Indenturewhatsit, now it's your turn to help us,' said Harry.

'Yes, indeed; we have already re-charted our course. We are accelerating the Orb, and have plotted a new course that will take you right to the Leaf Star Triple V Docking Station for your maximal convenience, in exactly two days, thirteen hours and forty-one minutes. Hub Prime days that is, of course.'

'Hub Prime days?' said Harry.

'Ah yes, I forgot, you're from – what was it? Dirt?'

'No, Earth, thank you very much!'

'Whatever. Well, Hub Prime is an artificial planet built over the black hole at the centre of the galaxy, from which the Imperium is governed – though not us, we're not in the Imperium, in fact we're… actually, that's another story. Anyway, its day and night were both set at ten hours. Nice regular time, which became the timekeeping norm for the rest of the galaxy.'

'Oh, I see,' said Harry, 'like Greenwich Mean Time?'

'I expect so, yes,' said the ambassador, 'but vastly more important, governing the lives of billions and billions and billions of intelligent organisms and entities spread all around the huge vastness that is the galaxy, rather than, let's say for instance, some tiny, insignificant little village on a backwater planet in the middle of nowhere called Dirt.'

'Earth! But yeah, I get it,' said Harry as the twins put their hands up to their mouths and giggled.

'Anyway,' said Ambassador Dee-Ung, 'you can Decouple the Gravitronic Grapple now, everything is ready.'

Harry paused. 'How do we know you've done what you said you've done?'

'Oh, please, a Deal's a Deal, as I've said. Anyway, if I didn't keep my part of the bargain, the Indenturesite would shrivel up and die.'

'How can I tell if it's still there?' said Harry.

'Think about it,' said Dee-Ung.

'What?' said Harry.

'My worm. Imagine it in your head, nestled somewhere close to one of your horrible palpitating organs, hanging off one of your vile, alien-shaped skeleton bone-things.'

Harry thought about the little brown worm. Immediately he could feel it. It was like a tiny little Coagulite, speaking to him with the ambassador's voice, saying, 'A little piece of Dee-Ung is here.'

Every time he thought of it, it said the same thing. Harry shuddered in disgust. He'd do his best not to think about it at all if he could!

'Anyway, enough jibber-jabber, Meatstick! Cut those grapples!' said the ambassador.

'Right,' said Harry. 'Here we go. Computer, turn off the Tractor Grapple thing!'

'Disengaging Gravitronic Grapple,' said the computer.

'Thank you, Captain Harry. Farewell…for now.' And the ambassador raised a gooey tentacle and waved it before oozing back into the comet ship. The hatch slammed shut, and then the Inscrutable Ballistic Orb shot away and out of sight with incredible speed.

Harry, Gaggenow and the twins stared at the galaxy ahead of them. They were hurtling back towards it at an unimaginable speed. Slowly, ever so slowly, it began to grow in size.

'I'm knackered,' said Harry.

'Yes, me too,' said the twins.

'Indeed,' said Gaggenow. 'Time for bed. And now I'll be able to choose a stateroom of my own – I think the Luxury Guest Cabin. Yes, that should be suitable for the Great Gaggenow!'

'Hold on, where am I going to sleep?' said Harry.

'Hah, you can have my mattress in the Scrap Metal Hold; I won't be needing it any more!' said Gaggenow.

'What? No way!' said Harry.

'The Captain's Cabin has been successfully reconditioned for your use, Captain Harry,' said the computer.

Harry turned to Gaggenow. 'Captain's Cabin,' he said. 'So there.'

Gaggenow made a face. 'Bah, it is of no consequence; I am still the Great Gaggenow, who sleeps in luxury tonight!' And with that he bounced out of the room.

'I'll be'

'off too,' said the twins.

'OK,' said Harry. 'I'll see you in the morning – things turned out all right in the end, didn't they?'

'Yes, they did.'

'It's lucky you'

'had us on board'

'to advise you, Earth boy,' said Alph and Bet.

'Right, of course,' said Harry sarcastically. 'Well, goodnight, then.'

'Goodnight,'

'Captain,' they said, before descending into gales of mocking laughter as they sauntered off down the corridor, arm in arm.

Harry sighed. The computer showed him to the Captain's Cabin, using a solid light hand that floated in the air to point the way. Harry was kind of pleased to note that it was now a human hand, and not a Grey hand. It seemed to him that the computer was the only real friend he had on the ship.

10 OWNED

THE Captain's Cabin was at the top of the ship, near the bridge. A large door, covered in Grey script, swished open as he approached. It was quite spacious inside. There was a cupboard full of strange things – tool belts, harnesses and science-looking waistcoats, obviously clothing for the Grey captain and a touch too small for Harry, and in any case, actually kind of weird. The bed was pretty comfortable, considering.

On one wall was a large monitor or TV screen. Which was odd. Why would the captain need that, when most monitors were generated by the computer holographically? Against another wall was a kind of curved console, with a really comfortable-looking hi-tech chair. Various instruments and readouts covered a large panel on the wall.

Harry walked over and sat in the chair. Immediately, a thin wire with a tiny metal ball on the end dropped into his lap.

'Sorry,' said the computer. 'Recalibrating for human use.' And the little ball rose up a bit to hover in front of Harry's mouth.

'What's that?' he said, and to his astonishment his voice echoed loudly all around the spaceship.

'Ship's Tannoy,' said the computer.

'Right,' said Harry. 'I get that.' Again, his voice boomed around the ship.

A voice came out of a little speaker on the table in reply. It was Gaggenow.

'Can you shut up, you cretinous caveman? I'm trying to sleep here!' he said.

'Sorry, sorry,' said Harry. Again, his voice echoed all over the place.

'Please be quiet,'

'stupid Earth boy,'

'I'm trying to'

'get some beauty sleep!' said the twins from another speaker.

'But how do I turn it off?' said Harry to everyone

and everything on the ship.

'Just say "Tannoy off", all right?' said Gaggenow. 'Really, I should be in charge – you don't know anything!'

'Tannoy off!' said Harry, irritated and embarrassed all at the same time.

'There are documents on the table that it is necessary for you to reassign,' said the computer. The computer used a solid light hand to point at a rectangular, shiny, granite-like slab resting on the table. Harry picked it up. The surface flickered into life, revealing a crisp screen. On it were displayed various words in Grey, as well as a revolving 3-D image of the Grey captain. The whole thing looked really cool and very fancy.

'What is it?' said Harry.

'Ship's Log and Certificate of Ownership.'

'Ship's Log, eh?' said Harry. 'How do I check that out?'

'It's the icon on the top right. Hold on. Switching to Earth English…' said the computer.

Words appeared on the screen in English. Harry was able to access the Captain's Log; it seemed that his name was Recon Team Leader Wirdle 112. The crew had similar names – Wardle 216, Wordle 1456, Wurdle 7562, Werdle 1433 and so on. All variations on Wordle/Wirdle etc. How confusing was that!

It turned out that the ship had left Canus Prime – the Greys' Homeworld – on a 'Covert Insertion Mission' to Yureshto, with a cargo of 'Infiltration Clones: Yureshtian Royal Twins, Alpha 45831 and Beta 45832'. They were authorised to visit Hub Prime and then Earth, where they were to perform a local 'Clone Candidate Harvesting Mission' before moving on to Yureshto and delivering the twins.

Harry saw an icon labelled 'Hub Prime Photo Album'. Curiosity piqued, he tapped it – and it opened up just like on one of those tablet things back home.

Harry raised an eyebrow. Judging by the photos, the Hub Prime visit was nothing more than a bit of tourism. A holiday, basically. There were pictures of various Greys standing outside tall buildings and enormous monuments straight out of a science fiction blockbuster film, and of Greys sitting in

bars with silly hats on and large multi-coloured drinks in their hands. The twins were in some of them too. One picture particularly drew Harry's attention. It was labelled 'Imperial Regalia' and it showed the captain and a couple of other Greys standing in front of an awesome collection of crowns, sceptres, rods, orbs and suchlike, really not very different from the Crown Jewels in the Tower of London back home on Earth, except instead of being owned by the Queen of England, they were owned by the Emperor of the Galaxy – whoever he, she or it was. One thing stood out – a huge, brightly glowing jewel, about as big as an over-sized tennis ball, set atop an ornate crown. Apparently the jewel was called the 'Crown Starheart' and was famous all over the galaxy.

Harry frowned. Who was that in the background? It appeared to be some kind of janitor or uniformed attendant, but it seemed strangely familiar. Harry used his fingers to enlarge the pic. And again… There! That face. It was…yes, it was, it was Gaggenow! Looking as shifty as anything. Mind you, he always looked shifty, but still. What was he doing there? Scoping out the Greys and their ship, presumably. Hub Prime must have been where he stowed away on the ship.

The computer interrupted his thoughts. 'Excuse me, Captain, but ownership of this ship must be reassigned to you,' it said.

'To me! Really?' said Harry.

'Yes. Please touch the icon labelled DNA Sampling,' said the computer.

Harry duly touched the screen. He felt the briefest of flashes, and then the screen began to swirl and pulse with light. Moments later it was his face on the screen, revolving in 3-D. Below it, these words appeared in PanGal, but the computer translated them into English for Harry.

CERTIFICATE OF OWNERSHIP
Deep Recon Wheelship Model Type
AG85CLE-FW569
Name: <Field Requires Input>
Owner: Captain Henry Greene
System: Sol.
Planet: 3 (Earth)
DNA code verified.

Harry stared in wonder. How cool was that!!!

'Ship name required,' said the Computer.

A name! What was he going to call it? It could be anything, anything at all. What was that name he'd given to his mate Harvey's biggest, bestest battleship in *Astropocalypse*?

'Oh yes, *Fartface Banana Nose*!' said Harry out loud.

'SS *Fartface Banana Nose* it is, then,' said the computer. Harry's jaw dropped in horror as the words appeared on the Certificate of Ownership: 'Starship *Fartface Banana Nose*'.

'No, no,' he said. 'I was just joking, we can't call it that!'

'Ship name has been assigned. Cannot be reassigned until ownership changes, either through death of captain, or sale of ship,' said the computer.

'Oh, great,' said Harry. 'I'm the captain of the *Fartface Banana Nose*...'

He went over to the captain's bed, and sat down with a sigh. He was such an idiot sometimes. And then, on a side table, he noticed a crumpled-up...something. It was like paper, except that it wasn't. It was as thin as paper, if not thinner, but as he unfolded it and spread it out, it lit up like a tablet. It had pictures and text and stuff he could enlarge or activate with his finger. Basically, it was a super-thin tablet, and seemed to be some kind of newssheet. And this what it said:

THE SUPERNOVA[1]
Gossip Column   21.8.4056 GMT

With Colum the Columnite Columnist from the planet Caryatid, Supernova's *favourite gossip hound! Even if she is a bit stony-faced — she rocks when she writes, oh yes![2]*

Boobleflops[3], everyone!
Boy, have I got some gossip for you! Bounty hunters and food fads, it's all here in this week's super-sized, super-cool, super-awesome Supernova*!*

New Taste Sensation Sweeps the Empire
It's called 'Toast'. Apparently discovered on some backward, pre-space flight, primitive planet in a far-off, remote section of the galaxy, 'Toast' is made by 'toasting' or lightly charring both sides of a foodstuff made from the seeds of plants that have been ground up into a fine

---

1 *The* Supernova *is a fully owned subsidiary of the Wagglestaff Corporation*

2 *Apologies for appalling puns.*

3 *'Boobleflops' — a phrase used by the Columnites of the planet Caryatid, denoting a gleeful, but also absurd and rather surreal greeting.*

powder, reconstituted with liquids and salts and then baked. Then you cut it up and burn it a bit. I mean, where do they come up with this crazy stuff? Tastes delicious with a bit of Smogpus butter and some Farglian Roach Jam. Apparently.

Tiny Tin is on his way!

Tiny Tin, the renowned robot bounty hunter, has announced his intention to hunt for the criminal known as Gaggenow. The bounty is a whopping one million Galactic Credits, dead or alive  (preferably dead). Watch out, Gaggenow, or whatever your real name is, Tiny Tin is coming to get you! Tiny Tin is so nicknamed because he's actually not really very tiny, and not made of tin. In fact, he's eight feet tall and made of titanium. But you know what those bounty hunters are like – all wry humour, big guns and handcuffs. Service with a smile, eh?

Smurglesnots[4] until next time, alien freaks!

---

4 Loosely translated as 'Farewell, and don't eat the yellow snow.'

A bounty hunter – that didn't sound good. An eight foot tall robot. After Gaggenow – which also meant it'd be after him and the twins! They'd have to be on their guard, even if they were on the edge of the galaxy.

Bet he knew about this all along, thought Harry. *The little sneak!* But then another thought struck him. Toast. He fancied some, sure, but that wasn't the point. Toast – that had to come from Earth, right? Had to! Harry stared at the picture of Colum the Columnite. She looked like some kind of weird crystal or rock-based alien. Whatever she was, he had to find her.

Whoever had told her about toast knew where Earth was…

11 CABIN FEVER

HE woke to the sound of girlish laughter ringing in his ears. Harry sat up, feeling a wave of despondent gloom washing over him. There was a big English test at school today, and he knew he was going to fail it. He looked around with bleary eyes. What was that against the wall…some kind of super flash computer console? Not only that, his room looked like it had been redecorated – in shiny, smooth grey steel with black trim, a bit like some kind of uber hi-tech alien spaceship or something. And was that a pair of bluish ankles disappearing around the corner of the door? And who was giggling? Was that Harvey's sister, Molly, laughing at him?

Grey steel? Blue-skinned ankles???

Harry sat up as it all came back to him in a rush. The feeling of despairing drudgery gave way to an excited surge of adrenaline. Blue skin – the cloned alien twins, of course, no doubt laughing at him as he slept. It was just the sort of thing they'd do. Grey steel? He was in the Captain's Cabin on a spaceship, of course. His spaceship! Yesterday had been one helluva fourteenth birthday for a certain fellow called Harry Greene, one he wasn't going to forget in a hurry! Or rather, Harry Greene: Starship Captain.

Harry couldn't help himself and he grinned a huge grin. Harry Greene: Starship Captain. Awesome. Captain of the *Fartface Banana Nose*, no less, and he burst out laughing. He began to review yesterday's events, a catalogue of wonder, adventure, terror, fear and joy. So much more interesting than his dull life back home, where he lived on a council estate, and went to school where a big bully and his gang wanted to flush his head down the toilet. And what would his mate Harvey think of all this? Would he be missing him? His mum would be, for sure! Harry wished he could talk to her, reassure her, down there on Earth. Or Dirt, as that weird alien had called it, heh, heh. Suddenly, a voice sounded inside his head: 'A little piece of Dee-Ung is here.'

'Whoa!' said Harry, shuddering with disgust. The Indenturesite whatsit! Best not to think about that. He leaped out of bed, putting parasitical blob worms out of his head, ready for a new day. Though for now, he could really do with a wash. And a visit to the toilet.

'Computer, where's the bog?' said Harry.

'En suite Comfort Station available here,' said the computer. A big hand appeared out of nowhere, now apparently encased in a white glove, and began jabbing at a section of the wall. A hidden door swept open as Harry approached, leading to a clean, all-white super hi-tech bathroom. Ten minutes later, Harry was all spruced up and clean and heading for the door. Time for breakfast!

Harry walked past the large monitor screen on the wall…and noticed that it appeared to be hot, with a soft residual glow. Obviously, it had been turned on and used very recently. He frowned. Looking closer, he saw a small off/on button. Intrigued, he pressed it. The monitor flickered into life – to show exactly what Harry was seeing! He was watching the monitor, with his hand resting on the button, and that's what the monitor showed, and over into infinity, just like the time he was lying on that slab surrounded by Greys.

Harry tried remembering something... He was at school, and Todd Scarswell's elder sister, Leanna, and her mates Jasmin and Zara had snatched his MP3 player and were scrolling through his playlist, taking the mickey out of his music. That had really upset him, as it was his mum who'd put him onto half of the tracks. Sure, they were mostly 'oldies' but it was one of the few times he and his mum actually sat down together and shared stuff, so it was precious to him. Their mocking laughter really hurt, worse than a kicking from Scars and his gang.

Sure enough, the memory appeared on the monitor, crisp and new-looking, as if it were some kind of high school soap opera in HD. Harry put a hand up to his chin, puzzled.

'Computer,' he said, 'why does this monitor show my memories like this?'

'Monitor is a Neuronological Energy Capture Device, used for reading and copying the memories of Clone Candidates.'

'Yeah, I kind of guessed it was something like that, but why is it still showing my memories?'

'Neuronological Prosthesis has been surgically implanted in your brain. Whenever you are near such a device, any memories you bring up will be displayed.'

'Can it be removed?' said Harry.

'Affirmative,' said the computer.

'Computer, remove Neuronological Prosthesis,' said Harry.

'Unable to comply,' said the computer. 'Requires Surgeon or AutoDoc trained or programmed to Level 16 Indigenous Earth Biology, subset: Primates

– *Homo sapiens.*'

Harry frowned. That was two weird things inside him that he'd have to get out somehow. But for now, there was nothing he could do about it. Harry shrugged.

'Oh well, time for breakfast,' he said, and headed off to the galley.

There he found Gaggenow and the twins, munching their way through bowls of that grey, rather sour-tasting stuff they called Nutrit Porridge. As soon as he walked in, the girls looked up, turned to each other and giggled.

Harry sighed resignedly as he sat down. 'Good morning, Alph and Bet,' he said. 'Morning, Gaggenow.'

The girls nodded. Gaggenow barely acknowledged him. Gaggenow had extended a long, thin, tubular tongue into his bowl of porridge and was sucking it up noisily. Harry stared in horrified disgust. His tongue was basically a straw. A pink, wet, glistening straw. Yuck! Harry continued to watch him eating – or was it drinking? – fascinated and revolted all at the same time.

Gaggenow reeled his tongue in like a strand of spaghetti, and said tetchily, 'What? What is it?'

'Oh, sorry, nothing, nothing,' said Harry, picking up a spoon, wondering to himself whether or not to ask Gaggenow to wear the Holographic Harness when he was eating.

'Where's that holo-harness thing?' said Harry.

'Broken,' said Gaggenow. 'By you, actually, with your fat ape fingers.'

'Oh, right. Ah...well, sorry about that.' Harry decided to change the subject. 'Anyway, how long before we reach that space station?'

'The Leaf Star Triple V? Tomorrow. Well, I say tomorrow, but there's no real night and day out here, so I mean after the next Sleep Cycle,' said Gaggenow.

'And what happens then?' said Harry.

Gaggenow put a bony four-knuckled hand up to his face, and stroked his chin ruminatively.

'Well...' he said, 'I guess we'll have to wait and see, but I intend to get on with my life. I have things to do, people to see, places to hide – I mean go! Places to go!'

'Yeah, I bet you do,' said Harry. Harry handed him the *Supernova* gossip column, jabbing a finger at the picture of the bounty hunter.

'Tiny Tin is after you!' said Harry.

Gaggenow's face went a strange shade of pale indigo, and he gulped, before putting his hands over his eyes. It seemed Gaggenow had had no idea about Tiny Tin after all!

'What?' said the twins.

Harry grinned. 'Bounty hunter…after him. And us, too, probably.'

The twins blinked their big golden eyes at him in horror.

'Hardly surprising,' said Harry, 'what with that big reward and all – why are they after you, anyway?'

Then Gaggenow seemed to get a hold of himself, and he blustered, 'Oh, nothing, nothing, it's all a misunderstanding. Different Gaggenow and all that. And don't worry! I am not called the Great Gaggenow for nothing, you know. I can outwit Tiny Tin. And before you even think about trying to turn me in for the reward…'

Harry put his hand up, and interrupted, 'Hey,

Gaggs, I wouldn't do that, really I wouldn't.'

Gaggenow stared at him, fish eyes narrowed in suspicion. 'Riiight. Of course you wouldn't!'

'No, really, Gaggs, I wouldn't! Not after what we've been through together!' said Harry, and he meant it, of course.

'Well, whatever. In any case, where we're going, it's a Triple V. Too far out for bounty hunters or GalPol. There'll be security, of course, but company security, not the real deal. Oh, and the name's Gaggenow, preferably the Great, or the Magnificent, not "Gaggs"! Really, show some respect,' said Gaggenow.

'Yes, quite so,'

'show some respect,' said the twins.

'Oh! And I suppose I should be calling you two your most royal highnesses, the Tsare-whatsits Alph and Bet, eh?' said Harry.

'Tsarevna. And yes,'

'of course, that's my'

'proper name and title,' they said.

'But you don't have to call me Captain, though, right?' said Harry.

'Oh no,'

'naturally not'

'as you are a commoner,' said the twins.

'Not to mention a primitive primate from an undeveloped backwater of the galaxy!' added Gaggenow, which made the twins giggle.

'How do you even know that?' said Harry, irked.

'I've been there, remember?' said Gaggenow.

'What, at the North Pole – you think the whole place is like that?'

'No, no, I just said that because it was the first place that popped into…well, anyway, I've been to several of your large, sprawling, stinking, filthy, barbarian-infested cities, believe me. Vile!'

Harry frowned. 'What were you doing there, anyway?' he asked.

'Best place to hide… I mean…err…tourism! Yes,

tourism. Well, work, that is. For a tourism outfit, you know, for a holiday company. There's lots of money in primitive holiday visits, seeing what the funny little natives are up to with their capering and jolly dancing, and their cute little arts and crafts and weird cuisine.'

'Uh-huh,' grunted Harry. 'And did you try some toast whilst you were there?'

'Toast! Ah, I see, you think the primitive planet they're talking about is Earth. Hmm, could be, I guess,' said Gaggenow.

'But this article here – other people, aliens and that, they've visited Earth?' said Harry.

'I would think so,' said Gaggenow.

'Anyone know where the *Supernova* is based? You know, where the offices are? Where this Colum works?'

'No, we are far too'

'high class to read'

'that sort of thing,' said the twins.

Gaggenow shook his head. 'Sorry, no.'

Harry sighed, and fell silent.

'What about you, Harry, what will you do when

we get back to civilisation?' said Gaggenow.

'I want to go home, really, make sure my mum's OK, tell her I'm alive. Trouble is, I don't know where Earth is! So I'm going to take the ship and look for it. I think Colum the Columnite might know where it is – if I find her, I can find Earth,' said Harry.

'Take the ship…' said Gaggenow. The twins' eyes widened just a touch and they began to blink their weird blink.

'Yes,' said Harry. 'Why not? I am the captain, after all, and I really would like to get home.'

Gaggenow and the twins exchanged a look. Harry frowned.

'What's the problem?' he said.

'Oh, nothing, nothing,' said Gaggenow, looking at the back of his hand, as the twins shrugged a noncommittal shrug.

'I mean, you can come with me, right? It'd be fun!' said Harry enthusiastically. 'And when we find Earth, maybe you could hide there again, Gaggs, try some toast. Or something. And you two, you could…well…hmm…I don't know…' said Harry and his voice tailed off as he began to realise how difficult it would be for them to actually live on Earth. 'Maybe…well, maybe some holo-harnesses or something…'

'Sounds wonderful,' said Gaggenow insincerely. 'Anyway, that's something we can worry about later. For now, let us just enjoy the fact that we are not going to die alone in the Void and that soon we will reach civilisation!'

'In *our* wonderful ship, *AG85*,'

'as the Greys call it,' added the twins.

'The *AG85*? Hah, not very imaginative, are they, the Greys? I think we should rename the ship now that it is ours!' said Gaggenow.

'Quite so,'

'how about'

'the *Royal Tsarevna*?'

'That is a noble name, it is true, but why not call it after its greatest ever passenger? Me!! The *Great Gaggenow* is an excellent name for a ship.'

Harry shifted uncomfortably in his seat.

'The ship has already been assigned a new name,' said the computer.

Harry coughed. 'Anyway,' he said, 'I guess it's just

a question of whiling away the time until we hit the Leaf Star, right? Computer, do you have any games?'

'Hold on, what do you mean the ship has a new name?' said Gaggenow. 'Who named it?'

'The captain, as per standard Galactic Maritime Protocols,' said the computer.

'Really? What did you call it, then?' asked Alph.

'Ummm…well…it…I…the…' Harry's voice tailed off into an incoherent mumble.

Gaggenow gave an exasperated sigh. 'Computer! What is the name of this ship?'

'This ship is named the SS *Fartface Banana Nose*,' said the computer.

There was a stunned silence.

Harry stood up. 'Well, that was nice. I guess we should just find some things to do or whatever, until we arrive at the Leaf Star. See you later!' Casually, he walked out of the galley, whistling jauntily. Behind him, all was quiet.

12 A DREAM WITHIN A DREAM

THE next morning (or rather, as there was no sun to actually make it morning, the next Wake Cycle) Harry woke with a start. The twins were giggling again – in fact, they were in the room. Bet was making a run for it, and Alph had just turned off the big monitor on the wall, and was turning to run after her sister.

'Oi!!!' shouted Harry. 'What are you up to?'

Alph paused for a moment, and turned. She gave him that weird sideways blink, and then put her hand up to her mouth and giggled, before turning away and dashing out of the room. Harry leaped out of bed and after them. He could see them running away down the corridor.

'Oi, stop, you little sneaks!' he shouted.

They stopped for a moment, both of them turning around in perfect unison. Their eyes widened into big, glowing golden discs and each put a blue-skinned hand up to her mouth, pointing at him with her other hand, and began to giggle uncontrollably. Harry frowned and looked down… Oh no! There were no pyjamas on board, of course, so he'd gone to bed without any. He was naked – completely naked!

He groaned incoherently and dashed back into his cabin as quick as he could, blushing as red as a tomato. The door shut behind him with a swish, and he leaned his back against it, breathing hard.

Which of course caused the door to open again, and he fell back out into the corridor. At the sight of him naked on the floor, the girls doubled over, hugging their stomachs, and laughed, and laughed, and laughed.

Despondently, Harry picked himself up, and headed back inside. His humiliation was complete. He sat on the edge of the bed, listening to the twins' fading laughter. After a few moments he thought to himself, *Actually, it couldn't get any worse, so why bother? So they saw me naked. Oh well, it wasn't the end of the world – they were taking the mickey out of me most of the time, anyway, so what's the diff?* With that thought, he picked himself up, got dressed and headed for the door. And then a thought struck him.

'Computer, does that Neuronological Monitor thing show what you are dreaming as well?'

'Affirmative, all non-conscious thoughts, memories and dreams,' said the computer.

'So that was what they were doing,' said Harry out loud, 'they were watching my dreams!' Harry made a face. The whole idea made him feel very uncomfortable indeed. He'd thought nothing could be worse than falling over naked in front of them, but this was worse! It was like they'd… well…invaded his mind. Gone through his drawers without his permission. That kind of thing. It wasn't right; he'd have to put a stop to that. Then he had another thought.

'Computer, does the neuronological device record what it plays?' he said.

'Affirmative, all memories and dreams are stored in its databanks,' said the computer.

Harry stared at the monitor, a feeling of mounting horror rising in his stomach. 'Computer, play back the dream that Alph and Bet were watching just now.'

The monitor flickered into life. Harry saw his mother, alone and lost, struggling to pull herself out of a huge, black mudslide that had destroyed her house and engulfed her. The mud was up to her waist, and she could barely move. She held her arms up to the heavens in a gesture of hopeless despair, and wailed.

Harry's heart ached at the sight of it.

But then a bright light appeared in the sky, and down swept a little spaceship, with Harry riding on the back of it, dressed like an intergalactic superhero.

'Don't worry, Mother, I'll save you!' said the heroic Harry. 'I'm a Starship Captain.'

Harry raised his eyes. Why couldn't he have come up with something a bit more subtle? No doubt the twins would have found this hilarious.

The heroic Harry swept his mother up into his arms, and flew her away to the stars. 'Oh, thank you, son, thank you for saving me,' said his mum proudly.

'That's OK, Mum! It's what I'm here for. And now we have to save the earth!' Suddenly, the scene shifted, and Harry and his mum were in a new kind of spaceship, a really cool-looking battleship of awesome power, floating above London. Some kind of inter-dimensional portal opened in the sky through which boiled and threshed a horde of hideous alien creatures, like gleaming armoured squid, each with the head of Todd Scarswell, his archenemy and the chief school bully. Harry and his mum fought the evil alien hordes together, side by side, in an epic battle of heroic proportions.

Back in the real world, Harry put his head in his hands. The twins were going to have a field day with this… He looked back at the Neuronological Device through his fingers, unable to wrench himself away.

He and his mother were receiving medals from the head of the UN, the President of the United States and the Prime Minister, for defeating the 'Scars', as the aliens were called.

And then the President of the Galaxy came and asked Harry so save the galaxy from the terrible Scars. And Harry became an admiral in charge of a battle fleet, and he and his mum defeated the Scars, this time in an even bigger battle, and saved the galaxy as well. And then the President of the Galaxy gave him a medal. And the President had a daughter, a girl with blue skin and golden eyes. Her name was Alph. And Admiral Greene went for walks with this girl, in a beautiful wooded wonderland…

In the real world, Harry began to feel sick with embarrassment. This couldn't be happening!

And in the dream, they held hands. And then

they stood together in a kind of flowery gazebo on top of one of those elvish trees from the *Lord of the Rings* films and gazed into each other's eyes. And kissed.

Harry leaped to his feet. 'NOOOooooooo!' he shouted.

And then it ended, as a peal of girlish laughter filled the sky, which was what had woken Harry up, in fact.

Harry couldn't believe it. This was terrible, truly awful. They'd seen all that… Alph had seen it! He couldn't bear it, he just couldn't bear it. If he saw them, he'd turn into a huge, red, blushing tomato. He'd explode with embarrassment, spraying tomatoey stuff all over the walls. And if they told Gaggenow – oh, the shame! There was nothing for it, he'd just have to stay here in this cabin until… well. For ever.

Harry shook his head. That was no good.

'Pull yourself together, Harry,' he muttered. He wasn't going to let two little jumped-up, self-important, arrogant so-called princesses keep him cooped up in here for ever! No. He had things to do. It might have been a dream, but actually his mum really did need rescuing, and he really was a starship captain! There was nothing for it but to pretend that he hadn't seen the dream, that he didn't know anything about him and Alph and that he really, absolutely, emphatically did not fancy her! And anyway, why Alph and not Bet? Well, whatever, forget about that. And as for falling over naked in the corridor... Hah! Compared to the dream, that was nothing. He could live with that, easy.

Harry straightened his shoulders and hardened his heart. He'd front it out, right in their faces. Remember, he said to himself, you are Harry Greene: Starship Captain!

With that thought in his head, he strode off down the corridor like he owned the place. Which, in fact, he did.

13 THE LAST RESORT

HARRY was sitting in the captain's control chair on the bridge. Behind him and to either side stood Gaggenow and the twins. Ahead of them, through the viewing window, a host of stars was spread out across the firmament: numberless, endless, awe-inspiring. A single star picked itself out from the multitude, a dull red one. It began to grow, getting larger and larger all the time as they hurtled towards it at enormous speed.

'At this rate we'll plummet right into the heart of the sun – are you sure this is right?' said Gaggenow.

'We're decelerating all the time and the computer says we've got enough fuel to come to a halt; we should be fine. And it said that it was a red giant – big, but not nearly as hot as other stars, so don't worry too much about its size,' said Harry.

'Can we really trust that Coagulite ambassador,

though? What if he's just sent us off to the nearest big star, just to get rid of us?' said Gaggenow.

'I know, I know,' said Harry, 'but then again, that little bit of stuff…it's still there, inside me. Would he have gone to all that trouble if…?'

'Wait!'

'What's'

'that?' said Alph and Bet.

A small black dot appeared, silhouetted against the vast shimmering redness of the star. It began to grow at an alarming rate and soon it had resolved itself into a huge object of gleaming silver and green. The green was bright, vibrant, which gave an effect as of a living plant. In fact, the whole thing looked to Harry like a kind of beautifully constructed leaf, hanging in space. Maybe even an oak tree leaf.

'I know it's called the Leaf Star, but I didn't think it would actually look like a leaf,' said Harry.

'Why not?' said Gaggenow. 'It's a space station that never moves, floating in space. It can be whatever shape you like, so why not something arty?'

'I think it'

'looks lovely,' said the twins.

Harry had to agree. The whole thing had a Christmassy feel about it, like a fresh green leaf hanging off a bright red bauble.

'Incoming Message,' said the computer. A large holographic monitor appeared in the air. The screen flickered into life, and a face appeared staring down at them. The face was covered in white fur but with recognisable features as far as Harry was concerned – two eyes, a kind of nose, a mouth, three big front teeth. And big floppy ears. Harry blinked in astonishment. It looked just like that character from *Alice in Wonderland*. Who was it?

'The white rabbit!' he blurted out loud.

'What? No, he's from the planet Orycto. An Oryctonite, in fact,' said Gaggenow. 'Bureaucrats, through and through.'

'Greetings; I am Harbourmaster Naknok of the Leaf Star Triple V Resort,' said the rabbity Oryctonite. 'I see two royal Tsarevnas of Yureshto, and an Ichthysupial, but you, in the captain's chair… you're not from around here, are you?'

'No, I'm a human. From Earth.'

'Hmph, never heard of it. And your name?'

'Harry. Captain Harry.'

'Harry? Curious name. And where is this…planet, what was it – planet Mud?'

'No, Earth! And Earth is…well, somewhere over there,' Harry said, pointing vaguely at the rest of the galaxy.

'And I am the Great Gaggenow,' said Gaggenow. 'Captain Harry…well, in effect, he is my employee. I am the senior here; you may discuss our docking arrangements with me.'

'Hey, that's not true, I don't work for you!' protested Harry.

'Be quiet, and let me do the talking, cave boy!' hissed Gaggenow.

'No!' said Harry. 'I'm the captain, not you!'

'Well, whatever,' said Naknok emphatically, 'your approach speed is far too high, and your docking trajectory is out of kilter and highly unsafe. And as for discussing docking, let me be clear: you do not have clearance to dock. The pleasure liner SS *Bliss* is closing in to dock even as we speak. We're not accepting some unannounced heap of junk from the Void! Well not until the *Bliss* is docked and all the correct protocols have been followed. Not to mention the forms.'

'Heap of junk? It's a state-of-the-art Wheelship, if you don't mind,' huffed Gaggenow.

'Anyway,' said Harry, 'we're quite badly damaged, and I don't think we could stop even if we wanted to.'

'What? Your ship is – hold on, scanning... scanning... the SS *Fartface Banana Nose*? What the...?'

'Yes, well, that's what happens when you put a cave boy in charge,' muttered Gaggenow.

Harry glared at him.

The harbourmaster went on, 'Substantial damage to weapons and propulsion systems, hyper drive fuel drained...navigational effectuators at... Oh, my. And....well, the list goes on. Yes, there is a lot of damage indeed. What happened?'

'Leptira attack,' said Harry.

'Leptira, eh? Nasty!' said Naknok.

'I need emergency repairs immediately, refuelling and the like, and a nice suite of rooms at your charming resort,' said Gaggenow.

'Oh, you do, do you? And who's going to pay for all this?'

'I'm sure we can come to an arrangement,' said Gaggenow airily, as if he didn't even have to worry about money.

Harry was going to jump in and explain that it wasn't up to Gaggenow but suddenly he noticed something: a large liner up ahead, between them and the space station, presumably the SS *Bliss*. And they were heading straight for it.

'Umm...' he said. 'Computer, can we slow down please; we don't want to hit that, do we?'

'Attempting to retard speed, but propulsion system damage prevents effective braking in a timely manner,' said the computer.

'Oh, my, you're on a collision course. Evade, evade!' screamed Naknok.

The SS *Bliss* began to fill the screen. It was a huge spaceship, many times the size of the Greys' Wheelship.

The twins' eyes widened in fear. Gaggenow began to flap his big floppy feet, a sure sign he was starting to panic.

'Computer, avoid that ship,' screamed Harry.

'Attempting to change course...' said the computer. 'Firing retros... Response poor... Manoeuvring thrusters at fourteen per cent...'

Slowly, ever so slowly, the *Fartface Banana Nose* began to turn away, but it wasn't happening fast enough. They were getting closer and closer all the time. The *Bliss*, too, was attempting to turn, but it was huge and slow. Now they could see a row of observation portholes along the side of the big liner. Many faces – strange alien faces of all shapes, sizes and colours, some furry, some tentacled, some in tanks of liquid, some floating and so on – were pressed against the windows, staring at them in horror.

'You idiots, what do you think you're doing? Move, move!' screamed Naknok.

The ships drew together at frightening speed – Gaggenow sank into a heap, hands over his head, whilst the twins simply started screaming, eyes as wide as golden gongs. Harry stared up at the looming collision, thinking furiously, but nothing came to mind. Every second, though, the ship was turning, turning, lessening the impact. Maybe they might just make it, or perhaps land only a glancing blow that both ships could survive. Harry crossed his fingers.

Closer and closer the ships came, each desperately trying to turn away from the other. A klaxon began to sound, blaring loudly throughout the ship. Several instrument panels began to flash various alerts and warnings.

'Warning, Proximity Alert! Warning, Proximity Alert!' said the computer over and over again, until Harry said, 'Yeah, we know – enough already!'

And then they struck. The ship shuddered and shook, spilling Harry out of his chair. The twins fell sprawling in a heap of thrashing blue limbs – Gaggenow, though, was already in a heap, floppy feet and bony hands protecting his long, fishy head. The unfortunately named *Fartface Banana Nose* actually bounced off the side of the SS *Bliss*, and plunged straight toward the space station. The Wheelship came off worse – its hull was breached, but luckily for its crew, it was the hull of a cargo hold, and it was automatically sealed before any more damage could be done. The SS *Bliss* was badly scratched – nothing a decent paint job couldn't fix, though.

'You incompetent fools,' said Naknok. 'Now you're heading straight for us!'

By now, the *Fartface Banana Nose* had lost a lot of its speed, but still…a head-on collision with a space station. It would be bad.

'Haven't you got any Gravi-whatsit Grapples?' shouted Harry over the noise of the damage reports, alerts and warnings, as he struggled to his feet.

'Yes, of course, but that's only for docking!' said Naknok.

'Well, then, you're going to have use them to get us into the dock safely, aren't you?' said Harry.

'What? But you're not authorised. You haven't been cleared! You haven't paid any harbour fees, we don't know if your cargo is legal, or if your passengers have the right papers, we haven't even…'

'Warning: Proximity Alert,' said the computer. 'And this time it's serious! Space Station in the way!'

'Hear that, Naknok?' shouted Harry. 'You've got no choice. There's got to be some kind of emergency docking procedure, right? Use it, or we'll smash into you and we'll all get it in the neck!'

Gaggenow poked his head up from between his feet. The twins, meanwhile, were staring at the looming space station with their eyes as wide as golden suns.

Naknok stared at Harry for a moment. 'Ach, curse, blast and Fipton Mallets,' he said. 'There's no choice. Initiating Emergency Docking Procedures!'

Harry frowned. Fipton Mallets? The translator whispered in his ear. 'Fipton Mallets. A kind of swear word or curse in Oryctonese with no real direct translation. The closest earth approximation is "Bum Hammers of Doom", but that's not really right.'

Harry couldn't help himself, and he began to laugh.

Naknok's hands – furry, three-fingered, rabbity hands – were flying over some kind of keyboard console, desperately trying to bring the Wheelship under control. He looked up and said angrily, 'Oh, you think this is funny, do you? We'll see if you're still laughing after we hit you with the bill!'

Just then, five greenish beams of energy leaped

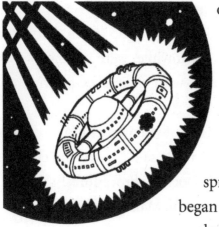

out from the space station to grab the Wheelship in a kind of energy vice. Once again, Harry and the twins were sent sprawling as the ship began to decelerate at an alarming rate. But the Gravitronic Grapples could only do so much, and they found themselves hurtling into a vast docking bay, many times their size. Ahead, huge energy buffers – kind of like the things you see at the end of railway lines, but made of enormous cushions of glowing green energy – awaited them. Everywhere, alarms, klaxons and warning lights were flashing. The Leaf Star's computer began to give out a warning of its own to the *Fartface*: 'I'm so sorry to bother you, sir, madam or thing, but your approach speed is a little too high. If you don't slow down a tad, you may sustain a nasty injury, and we wouldn't want that, would we? Not to mention the danger to our other guests!'

A lot politer than his own computer, probably because it was basically a five-star hotel computer and had to be nice to everyone, Harry found himself thinking, which seemed a stupid thing to be thinking as the ship was hurtling towards the far end of the docking bay for a rendezvous with certain death.

'Shut up, Con,' screamed Naknok, 'and divert all available power to the Energy Buffers, now!'

The entire Leaf Star went completely dark for a second or two, and the Energy Buffers began to swell up to twice their normal size, glowing brightly as they did so. A few seconds later, the ship slammed into the green, cushioning energy field – but it was like falling into a pile of mattresses or a big airbag. The ship sank into the buffers, slowing all the time, until it ground to a halt inches away from the far wall of the Docking Bay. The lights came back on all over the Leaf Star. Gaggenow, Harry and the twins let out a collective sigh of relief. Seconds later, the computer sighed in relief as well. Harry frowned. Was the computer taking the mickey?

And then the space station computer spoke.

'Welcome to the Leaf Star Resort. On behalf of Harbourmaster Naknok and all the staff, we would like to wish you a pleasant stay and a wonderful holiday. Thank you for choosing Triple V resort holidays and…'

'Shut up, Con!' said Naknok.

'Con?' said Harry. 'Funny name for a computer.'

'It's a Flabbergast Concierge, so Con is short for… What am I telling you this for? Your incompetence nearly destroyed this space station and all the people on board! I'll have you up before the Galactic Maritime Board for this. Have your licence stripped and your bum so sued you'll be paying damages for ever and ever until the end of time! I'll have you…'

'All right, all right, keep your fur on!' said Harry.

'What!!! How dare you, you little…' shrieked Naknok.

'Harbourmaster Naknok,' interjected Gaggenow, 'perhaps I can help. After all, it is hardly our fault that our ship was so badly damaged, after an attack by those ruthless space pirates, the Leptira. But more importantly, you saved us, didn't you? And the Leaf Star. Heroically, in fact! Saved us from certain death, out there in the empty, friendless Void, where we would have all perished, alone and unmourned. Surely the Maritime Board would commend you for your selfless act, commend you for aiding fellow spacefarers in need, as the Galactic Maritime Code says you should, not to mention the Triple V corporation. You just saved one of their resorts, a multi-billion credit operation; they should reward you, commend you for…'

'Well…you make a fair point, if somewhat laboriously,' said Naknok, a little calmer now. 'But still, you're going to have to pay. And compensate the *Bliss* for damages, and the cost of them losing this bay, which is the biggest and best on the Leaf Star, specifically designed for pleasure liners like theirs. And then your ship will have to be repaired, just so I can see the back of you, if nothing else, and that'll cost too! Assuming you have any money, of course. Have you?'

Harry gulped. The twins looked at each other's feet. Gaggenow, though, Gaggenow just said smoothly, 'Of course we have, plenty of credits, plenty!'

Harry and the twins looked over at Gaggenow in panic. Gaggenow made a tiny hand gesture and shook his head ever so slightly, as if to say 'shut up and go with me on this'. Naknok, though, narrowed his eyes in a rabbity expression of mistrust and suspicion.

'Yeah, right,' he said.

'But of course – after all, this is a Grey Wheelship. Hi-tech indeed, and hardly the cheapest of ships to buy – you know what the Greys are like. And our passengers – two Yureshtian Royal Tsarevnas. Do you think they would be travelling without the credits to keep them in the manner to which they are accustomed?'

Naknok's expression changed. 'That...actually makes sense,' he said.

The twins tilted their heads back and assumed an air of arrogant disdain, playing the role of princesses to the hilt, and doing it most convincingly. Which was, after all, what they were created to do.

'In addition, consider this!' continued Gaggenow. 'Why would the Leptira attack us if we didn't have cargo and credits and ransom money?'

'Well…yes, that makes sense too,' said Naknok, 'but what about your captain? The funny-looking alien from Mud or whatever it is? He doesn't look… right.'

'Oh, of course. He was merely appointed captain for the Royal Tsarevnas' entertainment. He is in fact merely a pet. A talking pet, that the princesses are fond of. It amused them to make him the captain, that's all.'

'Hah, I can believe that,' said Naknok.

Harry's jaw dropped. He stared up at Gaggenow, eyes blazing. The twins put their hands over their mouths.

'That's why he's so…rude,' said Gaggenow. 'He's not very bright, barely an intelligent being, in fact. Thinks he really is a captain – which is sort of the fun of having them as pets. Humans! They really are most amusing little things.'

Harry set his jaw. He so wanted to intervene. But if he did…what would happen? Would they get tossed right back out into space?

'I see! Right, right,' said Naknok.

'And,' continued Gaggenow, 'I, Gaggenow the

Magnificent, am the Tsarevnas' High Steward, responsible for their safety and comfort and so on. Remember, Naknok, you have also heroically saved two Tsarevnas of Yureshto. Their Royal Clan are likely to reward you handsomely!'

'Why, yes, yes, they should, how splendiferous!' said Naknok, his tone entirely different and thoroughly ingratiating now. 'Umm... Welcome. Welcome, Your Royal Highnesses, to the Leaf Star Triple V. I hope your stay will be pleasant and enjoyable!'

The twins nodded regally, as if receiving what was their due. Gaggenow smiled, winking at Harry and the twins. Harry stared back at him angrily, arms folded.

'If you could start on the emergency repairs that would be most helpful; we have an important schedule to keep,' said Gaggenow.

'Oh, of course, High Steward, of course,' said Naknok.

'And make the Royal Suite ready for the Tsarevnas and me,' Gaggenow added. At this, the twins beamed happily, fluttering their hands in expectant joy.

'Immediately, immediately!' said the harbourmaster. 'And what about Harry, the Royal Pet?'

'Oh, I think the Servants' Quarter, don't you?' said Gaggenow.

14 LEAF IT OUT

HARRY stared up at the stars spread out like a blanket of diamonds across the vastness of space. They stared back. No one spoke.

He was standing on one of the Leaf Star's Observation Decks. This part of the deck was known as Galside. The other, where the view was of a vast nothingness, was called Voidside. And at the end of the deck was Starside, where the huge red giant filled the entire viewing window like an enormous glowing ruby. The overall effect of these different views was really quite majestic, and Harry could fully understand why the Leaf Star had been built here. Nothing could match the sheer beauty of it all, and so clear too, not like the night sky back home. Back home... Harry sighed despondently. His mother would be in a terrible panic by now. After a day – well, maybe they'd have thought he was truanting. But after all this time? The police would have been called, social services and all the rest. They'd be trawling the local woods, where'd he run away the last time, and lived rough for a few days. And they wouldn't find him this time. He'd become a missing person, a face on a poster on a lamppost. His poor mum, she'd cry and cry.

But what would his mum think, if she really knew where he was? She'd be amazed. Harry looked around. The Observation Deck was full of hundreds of holidaymakers, of all sorts of sizes, shapes and hues. Creatures in tanks full of liquid, others with breathing aids, others that were breathing normally and yet more that didn't breathe at all but did... something else. Tentacles, claws, fingers. Single eyes, compound eyes, eyes on stalks. Mammal-like, lizard-like, insect-like, fish-like – you name it-like! Some were quite repulsive, some beautiful. Others were actually pretty terrifying, but Harry had learned that it was the height of rudeness to show any disgust or fear at the sight of another alien. After all, they were all aliens here.

Harry's stomach rumbled. Time for dinner. He

had to eat in the Servants' Galley – which meant, yes, you guessed it, more stinking Nutrit Porridge! Blast Gaggenow and his tricks! All right, he had to admit, Gaggs' fraudulent little scheme had worked – the ship was docked and being repaired, and they'd been allowed into the resort. It was just that it had worked out a lot better for Gaggenow and the twins than it had for him. Typical. And goodness knew what was going to happen when they found out there was no actual money. The Coagulite would really hit the fan then! Harry sighed. A bowl of Nutrit Porridge it was, then. And after dinner, he'd have to decide where to sleep. His room on the Leaf Star was a tiny servant's cabin, with a shared bathroom. Shared with a weird alien that was pretty much a giant man-sized slug. Whenever it went to the bathroom, it left a glistening trail of slime...

On the other hand, he could always go back to the *Fartface Banana Nose*, and sleep in the really rather comfortable Captain's Cabin. Except that the ship was undergoing twenty-four-hour continuous repairs. Well, twenty-hour (Standard Hubtime) continuous repairs, to be precise. It was overrun with Repair Droids and little rabbity engineers, and the noise was unbearable. He couldn't sleep through that.

As he walked on he spotted a little stand with what looked like balls of rolled-up newspaper. Harry picked one up and shook it out – it was a new edition of the *Supernova*.

THE SUPERNOVA[5]
Gossip Column   11.9.4056 GMT

With Colum the Columnite Columnist from the planet Caryatid, Supernova's *favourite gossip hound because she leaves no stone unturned! (Sorry, sorry.)*

Moggopalps[6], everyone!
Oh, my pebbles! The gossip, people, the gossip! It's all here in this week's super-sized, super-cool, super-awesome Supernova*!*

---

5 The Supernova *is a fully owned subsidiary of the Wagglestaff Corporation*

6 *Moggopalps – a phrase used by the Columnites of the planet Caryatid, denoting a greeting, but one mixed with affectionate derision.*

Anyone seen the Crown Starheart?

The greatest gem in the galaxy, the heart of a star itself, the Crown Starheart, ultimate jewel in the Galactic Overlord's Crown! Anyone seen it recently? The Office of the Vizier says it's been taken off display for cleaning, but I've heard something else! It's just a rumour, I know – a bit of gossip, but a little bird tells me that some people think it's been stolen… Can you believe that? Stolen from the Hub of the Empire itself, stolen from under the nose of the ruler of the Galaxy? Yeah, sounds ridiculous, doesn't it? Can't be true! Can it?

Burger Meat Scandal!

So…Astro Burgers. One of the biggest burger chains in the galaxy. You love 'em, right? Turns out they've been putting the wrong kind of meat in their burgers! Worse – sentient species meat! Traces of Grey, Fay and Oryctonite, to name but a few, have been found in the meat. GalPol has shut down their entire chain and arrested their Board of Directors, including the Galactic Magnate, the super-rich merchant, Fattus Baggus the

Shack, though Astro Burgers Corp is only a tiny part of his vast mercantile empire. The question is, where did they get the meat they've been adding to their burgers? Kidnapping people and killing them? Anyway, Supreme Lord High Devourer Bithyius of the Leptira has extended an offer to all Astro Burger Staff. 'They are welcome to set up again in Leptira space whenever they like. We love eating people!' said Bithyius.

Stankstinkmops[7] until next time, to all my alien fans!
(All Worlds Copyright © Wagglestaff Corporation)

Wow, those Leptira really are bad-ass, thought Harry. But it was the Starheart story that really interested him. There was a picture of it in his cabin, along with some Greys. And Gaggenow. As a janitor. And now it was…

Nah! Surely not. How could Gaggs have stolen that? Sure, he was a tricky little so-and-so, but there was no way he could pull off something like that! It'd be like Scars, his archenemy at school, stealing the Crown Jewels or something.

---

7 *Loosely translated as 'See you soon, but please wash your feet next time.'*

Ridiculous. But then again, there was that Tiny Tin bounty hunter character he'd read about in that earlier *Supernova*. Gaggs must have done something big to get that kind of attention! Harry looked up, half expecting to see the eight foot tall robot bounty hunter striding down the main thoroughfare of the Leaf Star. But no, everything was as you'd expect.

Still…it seemed so unbelievable! Harry shrugged, and set off down the deck to the exit. Up ahead, two blue-skinned figures approached him from the other direction – the twins, each holding a bag. A shopping bag, by the look of things. Harry stopped to stare for a moment. They were wearing new outfits – identical, of course. White toga-like dresses, cut above the knee, edged with gold, drawn in fetchingly around the waist with a golden belt. On their feet they wore white and gold sandals, with golden laces that wound around their calves, and on their heads, delicate tiaras of gold and silver, holding up their perfectly coiffured jet-black hair. On their hands were fragile fingerless gloves of white lace, held onto their wrists by wisps of golden thread. The whole thing had a bit of an ancient

Roman or Greek vibe about it. But with their bright blue skin, glossy ebony hair and golden eyes, the overall effect was, Harry had to admit, really quite stunning. They were beautiful. Annoying. Irritating. Treacherous, even. But beautiful.

The twins drew nearer, smiling disdainfully at him, as if they knew exactly what he was thinking. Harry pulled himself together – he was staring like an idiot! Then he began to blush. The girls sniggered behind their hands. Harry closed his eyes in despair. Blushing! It was so embarrassing.

'Ah, poor Harry, our gallant captain! We've come

to save you from the porridge; you can come and eat with us,' said Bet.

Harry opened his eyes, an expression of almost dog-like gratitude on his face. They were actually being nice to him! Well, Bet was, at any rate. He narrowed his eyes. She'd spoken on her own – what was going on? He looked at Alph. She merely looked down her nose at him and regally extended a gloved hand. Harry blinked at her, confused. Alph made a face and nodded at her hand. Ah, thought Harry, he was supposed to kiss it. She held it just low enough so that he'd have to bow down to do it.

Harry narrowed his eyes. 'No way,' he hissed.

'Yes way!' Alph hissed back, flapping her hand in his face. 'You peasant – look, people are watching.'

Harry looked around. Some tourists had indeed stopped to watch. After all, it wasn't every day you saw a pair of Yureshtian Royal Tsarevnas dressed in their full regalia parading round the deck. Harry bit his lip. Blast it, he was going to have to go along with it.

He drew himself up to his full height, bowed graciously, and lightly pecked the back of Alph's hand.

And then let a little bit of spit dribble onto her white, lacy glove.

Alph whipped her hand back in disgust – both twins glared at him, and for a moment looked like they were going to say or do something. Golden eyes flicked to either side. People were watching. In unison, they bowed and turned away as if nothing had happened. Then they pointed at their bags.

'Come, servant,'

'carry our bags'

'and follow us,' they said arrogantly.

Anger boiled up inside Harry – he so wanted to pick up those bags, empty 'em out on the concourse of the Observation Deck and scream at the top of his lungs, 'THEY'RE NOT PRINCESSES, THEY'RE JUST CLONES! CLONES, I TELL YOU. AND THEIR HIGH STEWARD IS A WANTED INTERGALACTIC CRIMINAL!' Instead he sighed, picked up the bags, and set off after them. He derived some satisfaction from the sight of Alph discreetly but frantically wiping the back of her hand with a gold-embroidered white handkerchief.

Ah well, he thought to himself, at least he'd be getting a decent meal.

Soon Harry found himself in the Luxury Class section of the Leaf Star. The floors were covered with soft, deep-pile carpets of imperial purple. Every corridor had blue-jacketed, red-capped servants at each end – a kind of furry monkey-like alien, but with four arms and four legs, perfect for carrying luggage and trays and drinks and so on. They came to a pair of huge golden doors, which opened silently at their approach.

The resort's computer, Con, spoke as they entered. 'Welcome, Tsarevna Alpha, Tsarevna Beta, and…err…'

'Insignificant Servant Harry,' said Alph.

'Ah… Insignificant Servant Harry,' echoed the computer. 'Welcome to the Royal Suite! I hope your shopping trip was pleasant and that the rest of your day will be good too!'

Normally that would have annoyed Harry and he would have made a face right back at Alph or something, but he was too staggered by the opulence of the Royal Suite to take notice. Everything was gold, or silver, or red, with magnificent paintings, hangings, curtains, four-poster beds, elegant chaise longues that floated on air and could be called over whenever you wanted them, and so on. And that was just the first room. There were so many more rooms.

'Put the bags'

'over there,' said the twins, pointing.

'Hah,' said Harry, 'no need to play that game any more.' And he dropped them where they were. 'Now, where's that meal you promised me?'

Bet nodded in the direction of one of the doors, but Alph folded her arms and said, 'So nice polite boy who knew his place has become rude Earth boy again, I see!'

'Yeah, well, rude Earth boy has been living off nothing but Nutrit Porridge for days and days and is desperate for something decent to eat!' said Harry, sauntering over to the door Bet had indicated. The door opened as he drew near, revealing a short corridor leading to a room marked 'The Banqueting Hall'. That sounded good!

He marched into the hall – it was long and high-ceilinged, and decorated like a Roman emperor's palace. A huge table filled most of the hall, and it in turn was filled with plate upon plate of food. Fruits, roast meats, vegetables of all kinds with a bewildering array of sauces, dips and condiments to go with them. None that he actually recognised, but Harry figured that if it was good enough for the twins, it would be good enough for him. They were basically human. Well, humanoid at any rate.

As he was about to tuck in, he heard voices from a side room off to the left. It was Naknok on the holo-monitor, and Gaggenow, deep in conversation. Something about the tone of their conversation drew Harry's attention. As quietly as he could, he crept over to listen outside the door.

'Yes, but the value of the Wheelship far outweighs the cost of the repairs and the tariff in the Royal Suite, doesn't it?' Gaggenow was saying.

'Oh, yes, indeed, High Steward Gaggenow, by several hundred thousand Galactic Credits,' said Naknok.

'Well,' said Gaggenow, 'all we need is passage – first class, of course – on a luxury liner to the nearest civilised planet within the Hub. We have no real need of the ship any more.'

'Really? But it's a Grey Wheelship!' said Naknok.

'Yes, but now that our diplomatic mission is complete – I cannot discuss the details, of course, you understand – the ship is an unnecessary expense,' said Gaggenow authoritatively.

'Yes, yes, of course. Now…well, let me see,' said Naknok. Harry could hear the sound of the harbourmaster's fingers working his keyboard.

'Ah… I can offer you a first class flight for four

– on the *Bliss*, in fact – to Haddus Prime, and from there to the destination of your choice, remission of all damages, docking, repair and hotel fees, plus two hundred thousand Galactic Credits for the SS *Fartface Banana Nose*,' said Naknok.

Harry's jaw dropped. That sneak Gaggenow, he was trying to sell the ship right from under his feet! Harry was all set to run in there and sort him out, and tell Naknok what was what, but thought better of it at the last moment. It could blow all their covers and they'd end up with nothing – if Naknok found out they had no money, he might seize the ship anyway. Well, whatever happened, he had to be on board the *Fartface Banana Nose*. He could control the ship from there, defend it even. Maybe even make a run for it…

The conversation between Gaggenow and the harbourmaster continued. 'Actually, we only need first class accommodation for three,' added Gaggenow.

'Oh, of course, that pet alien thing from Mud. Servants' quarters – be a lot cheaper,' said Naknok.

'Oh no, the human's services are no longer required

at all. You can have him – it – along with the ship,' said Gaggenow.

Harry shook his head in disgust. That little…

'All very well, but what would I do with it?' said Naknok.

'Oh, it's not entirely stupid. It'd make for a novelty servant. And at the very least, it can work in the galley or Waste Disposal or something,' said Gaggenow. 'And in any case, you are getting a generous deal on the ship, you'll be able to make a handsome profit – I'm sure you could do us a favour and take it off our hands.'

'Yes, yes, quite so, High Steward, quite so. I'm sure we can find a use for it,' said Naknok.

Harry ground his teeth. But he had to control himself and get back to the ship. With a monumental effort, he swallowed his rage, turned and quietly tiptoed away. Once he was out of the Banqueting Hall, he broke into a run.

'Hey! Where do'

'you think'

'you're going?'

'We haven't'

'finished playing with you'

'yet,' said the twins.

'Sudden fond desire for Nutrit Porridge after all,' said Harry as he ran out of the Royal Suite at top speed.

HARRY sat, or rather sprawled, in the captain's chair on the bridge of the *Fartface Banana Nose*.

'Computer, seal all the doors. Don't let anyone on board without my permission, OK?' said Harry.

'Righto, affirmative,' said the computer jauntily.

Harry sank his chin onto his chest, deep in thought. This one was going to require a plan. 'Computer, what is the status of repair?' he asked.

'Well, Harry, me old mate,' said the computer, 'ship has been fully refuelled and is

functioning at ninety per cent efficiency. Shields, Propulsion, Hyper Drive, Weapons, Life Support, Communications: all at one hundred per cent. Auxiliary systems such as the Replicators are still a bit knackered, though. Also, hull integrity is not at one hundred per cent. Medical Bay hull rupture has been fully repaired, but the Cargo Hold has been difficult for the Leaf Star engineers. It is still holed, but the Hermetic Force Bubble has sealed it off. However, this is causing a constant drain on the Fusion Banks, which could be a problem.'

Harry frowned. 'What's with you, Computer, you're talking like a human or something. What's going on?'

'Flabbergast 9-1000 built-in Sympathy AI. Over time, Computer – I – will learn to adapt to the captain. To sound more like him or her. Though the outcome is, of course, unpredictable, due to the nature of Neural Net Learning Processes.'

'Huh, cool!' said Harry. 'Does that mean you should have a name?'

'Yes, I suppose,' said the computer. 'How about Dave?'

'Dave? Really? Dave the super computer. Hah, OK then – Dave. So, Dave, could we fly off right now? I mean, the ship's operational and that?'

'Oh, yes,' said Dave the computer. 'It is fully operational. Just not for too long, with that energy drain.'

'Are they going to try and finish the hold repairs?' said Harry.

'No – all Leaf Star personnel and droids have left the ship. Their chief engineer said, and I quote, "I've had enough of this damned ship, and in any case, we haven't got an Uxian Ice Ale's chance in the centre of the sun of fixing it without more Canusium, and we're right out of that."'

'Uxian Ice…?' said Harry.

'A phrase denoting no chance at all, common to most Hub Worlds, but often regional, varying only in the type of Ale – Prime Ale, Bukosian Ale, Rigelian Ale, Aldebaran Ale, etc. An Earth equivalent might be "snowball's chance in hell",' explained Dave.

'And Canusium? What's that, and have we got any?'

'Oh, yes, and lots of it. It's a metal that only occurs

on Canus Prime, the Greys' Homeworld. Trouble is, we're using most of it: for the hull, the walls, the equipment. Me. So none left for repairs, I'm afraid, Harry,' said Dave.

Harry sighed. 'Right, so we'll have to risk that energy drain no matter what. Have we got enough power to get us away from here?'

'Yes, I have downloaded local Navigational Data from the Leaf Star. We could jump to Haddus Prime or Outpost 426.'

'Outpost 426? What's that?'

'No idea,' said Dave. 'All it says on the star chart is Outpost 426.'

'And Haddus Prime?'

'Inhabited by Haddusians. An ancient world whose surface has been scoured flat by aeons of high wind erosion. The Haddusians have evolved wheels instead of legs and a kind of sail made of a single leathery wing. They can reach quite high speeds!'

'Are they in the Hub?'

'No, they're independent, but they have underground mines where they harvest a kind of spice mould called Grerk. Highly prized by the Hub itself, so there is a big Hub Spaceport on Haddus Prime, entirely devoted to the trade in Grerk. Haddusians themselves – or Wheelies, as they are called – rarely leave their planet, as it's a lot of effort for them to get around – they need constant wind.'

'Hmph, weird! And that's it? Nowhere else? I thought the place would be crawling with planets, what with the number of weird alien types on the Leaf Star,' said Harry.

'Ah, but they are tourists, remember. We're out in the sticks here, on the edge of the galaxy. We're lucky to find anything at all that close. Of course, if we get nearer to the centre of the galaxy, to Hub Prime, then you will find it's "crawling with planets".'

Harry stared out into the vast docking bay of the Leaf Star. And made up his mind. Gaggenow had betrayed him utterly, and he was pretty sure the twins were in on it.

'Dave,' he said. 'Let's get out of here. Let's…blast off, or whatever it is.' As he said it, his heart sank. He'd be leaving…her.

'I'm afraid it's not so easy, Captain Harry,' said

Dave. 'We need permission from the harbourmaster. Mooring lines must be de-coupled, Stabiliser Fields released. Not to mention repair fees, harbour tolls and departure taxes and so on.'

'Oh!' said Harry. 'Right, of course.' Much as he hated to admit it, he actually felt a little relieved at that. Now he'd have to try something else.

'Well, it's obvious the Leaf Star has no idea about the dead-or-alive reward offered for Gaggenow. What if we told Naknok – would I get the reward?'

'Analysis suggests this is risky,' said Dave. 'The problem is the wording on the GalPol bounty notice. The phrase "Also, any other beings found with him should be deemed to be his accomplices and dealt with accordingly" could prove tricky. He'd be well within his rights to inform GalPol, clap you all in irons and impound the ship, which he might then claim in lieu of taxes and bills. He'd get the ship and the reward.'

'Just as well, I suppose,' said Harry. Even though Gaggenow had stabbed him in the back, big time, he still didn't feel quite right in handing him over to be executed or worse. For money. That didn't seem right.

'If I may ask,' said Dave, 'what is this all about?'

'Well, Computer…'

'Dave,' interrupted the computer.

'Err…yeah. Dave. You see, Gaggenow tried to sell the *Fartface Banana Nose* right from under my feet.'

'Really? How?'

'Well, to Naknok. For a bunch of credits.'

'But how? You have the Certificate of Ownership. It's DNA-configured and all above board and legal,' said Dave.

'Oh yeah, of course! But then again, Naknok doesn't know that. Hmm. Couldn't we just email Naknok a copy of the certificate?' said Harry.

'Using Galnet, you mean? Of course. Shall I do so?'

'Yeah. Let's see what that brings out of the woodwork!' said Harry.

'The woodwork?' said Dave. 'There is no wood on board this craft.'

'No, I…oh, never mind,' said Harry. 'Just send the damn Galnet thing.'

'Done.'

It wasn't long before Dave spoke again. 'A person

calling himself Gaggenow seeks permission to enter the ship. Also, two beings called Alph and Bet,' said Dave.

Wow, that was quick, thought Harry to himself.

'Shall I allow them on board?' said Dave.

'No! Let them sweat for a few minutes,' said Harry, relishing his moment of power. After a good quarter of an hour, Harry said, 'All right, Dave, let them in.'

A few moments later, Gaggenow swept into the Control Room, the twins stamping along behind him.

'How dare you keep me waiting like that, don't you know who I am?' hollered Gaggenow.

'And us!'

'We're royalty!' said the twins, golden eyes blazing with indignant outrage.

Harry couldn't help himself and just smirked at them. He was enjoying this!

'Pah! Enough of this; what have you got to say for yourself, you primitive earthling?' said Gaggenow. 'I mean, who do you think you are?'

That was too much for Harry. 'Who do I think I

am? I'm the captain of this ship, that's who! I'm the "Earth boy" who saved you from the Leptira! Who got us to this space station – safely! Not to mention the fact that I am the legal owner of this ship. That's who I think I am!'

Gaggenow and the twins' jaws dropped, stunned into silence by his outburst.

'And who are you?' continued Harry. 'Gaggenow? A wanted criminal! I'm sure there's people out there would love to know where you are! Police, mostly, not to mention a certain robot bounty hunter! And you two…clones! Just clones. No doubt the real

Yureshtian royal family would love to know about that too!'

'Oh!' huffed Alph, putting her hands on her hips. Bet, though, blinked uncertainly. Alph turned to Bet, and made a face as if to say, 'What?'

'Well, he did actually save us,' said Bet. 'And he is…you know…' But her voice tailed off under Alph's wilting glare.

'Now then,' said Gaggenow, 'let's just calm down here for a moment. This is all getting a little out of hand. We're all friends here, aren't we?'

'Are we?' said Harry waspishly.

'Yes, yes, of course we are,' said Gaggenow, all smiles. 'Come, come, my dear boy!'

Harry narrowed his eyes. He knew Gaggenow had tried to maroon him on the Leaf Star, and the sheer insincerity of his words made him feel sick, though of course, Gaggenow didn't know that he knew. No, let him dig himself deeper and deeper into a hole, and then he'd expose the fish-faced fraud in front of the girls. They'd realise *he* was the good guy then, and not Gaggs.

'Actually, I came here to make you a business

proposal. You see, I have been negotiating on our behalf the sale of this ship,' said Gaggenow.

'What!' said the twins together.

'No, wait, hear me out,' said Gaggenow.

'Go on, then,' said Harry. This was going to be good.

'You see, I also saved us by getting the ship repaired, and some rather fine rooms…'

'Saved you, more like. I got to sleep in a room with a giant slug!' said Harry.

'Yes, well, three out of four was pretty good, I thought,' said Gaggenow. 'The girls, well, they need their beauty sleep, they're delicate creatures, and so refined…' As he said this, he bowed to the twins, who much to Harry's disgust preened themselves like exotic cats. He half expected them to start purring.

'You, though – well, you're a hero! A tough, fighting lad. A warrior! I knew you could take it, and that you'd go along with it for the good of us all,' continued Gaggenow.

The shameless flattery was turning Harry's stomach, though it was fascinating to watch Gaggs in full flow. What a con man! Well, con…thing.

'But here is our problem. We're ensconced on the Leaf Star, comfortably. But we can never leave, for we have no means to actually pay for anything. So, the solution is simple: we sell the ship, which easily pays off all our debts and gets us first-class passage to wherever we want, plus forty thousand Galactic Credits left over to be shared between us all equally!' said Gaggenow.

'That's ten'

'thousand credits'

'each. Fantastic!' said the twins, golden eyes wide with glee.

'Well, arguably, you could say that you two constitute one share, but hey, let's be generous. Of course, ten thousand each,' said Gaggenow.

Harry sat in his chair, open-mouthed. For once he was actually lost for words. Gaggenow's cheek was astonishing. The sheer, bare-faced gall of it all. He'd overheard him selling the ship for much, much more than that! Ten thousand each…whilst Gaggenow would walk away with…what…one hundred and seventy thousand?

'Well, I think that's'

'an excellent solution.'

'Not only do we get ourselves out of'

'a tricky situation, but we come away'

'with some substantial funds.'

'Well done, Gaggenow!' said the girls, clapping their hands together in unison.

Gaggenow bowed. Harry shook his head in disbelief. He was about to point out a few home truths when suddenly Dave spoke. 'Alert! High Priority Message from the Leaf Star!'

16 AIEEEEE!

A holo-monitor popped into the air in front of them. Naknok's face appeared, looking really quite terrified.

'Gaggenow, what the hell's going on?' he shrieked.

'Why, what's happened?' said Gaggenow.

'Unidentified craft detected,' said Dave. 'Heading this way – fast!'

'That's what's happened,' said Naknok. 'It's a Leptira battle cruiser!'

'Confirmed,' said Dave. 'Leptira battle cruiser. Called…the SS *Mantid Raptor*. Hmm, sounds familiar somehow.'

Gaggenow's face turned a bright shade of yellow. 'Farglian fudge!' was all he could get out, before he sank into a heap, hands and feet covering his face.

The twins' eyes became golden orbs. They turned to Harry.

'What are we'

'going to do?' they said.

'Oh, I see, you're ready to listen to me now, when trouble comes knocking on the door?'

'Well, yes,'

'of course,' said the twins.

That actually made Harry feel pretty good, and he smiled. But then they went on.

'You are a'

'commoner after all'

'and that is your job'

'– to look after us.'

Harry rolled his eyes.

'Well, whatever,' said Naknok. 'I know what I'm going to do – Initiating Emergency Deport Procedure!'

'What? You can't!' wailed Gaggenow. 'What about our deal?'

'Deal, shmeal! There's a High Devourer on that ship called Clypeus, and he's told me in no uncertain terms exactly what they're going to do if we don't hand over your ship and its crew to them immediately!'

'And you gave in? Just like that?' said Harry.

'Yeah, just like that,' said Naknok.

'But this way you'll never get your fees, or get your hands on this ship, or anything!' said Harry.

'Look, Captain, we have to face facts here. We're a pleasure resort. We've got some firepower, sure, but that's a Leptira battle cruiser, Mantid class. We wouldn't have much of a chance, even if we wanted to fight. Which we don't. I mean, if we lost…they eat Oryctonites, you know, they've got a special recipe and everything!'

'Guys, sorry to interrupt, but the Stabilisers have been shut off, and the Energy Buffers set to repel. We're getting fired out of the Docking Bay like a… well, an Earth thing from an Earth thing – I'm sorry, Harry, I can't find a suitable Earth simile from my database,' said Dave.

'Don't worry about it!' said Harry. 'Can we make a run for it?'

'No,' said Dave. 'A Leptira battle cruiser is at least five times as fast as us.'

'Oh yeah,' said Harry, 'you told me that already.'

'Did I? When was that?' said Dave.

'Doesn't matter,' said Harry, thinking furiously. 'How the hell did they find us?'

'No time to worry about that now,' said Gaggenow. 'Just get us out of here!'

'What if we tried to negotiate?' said Harry.

'Sure, good luck with that!' said Naknok. 'Docking Bay doors are open. Goodbye!'

With that, the *Fartface Banana Nose* shot out of the Leaf Star and out into the black emptiness of space. Except that it wasn't entirely empty. Although still some way off, the Leptira battle cruiser *Mantid Raptor* was hurtling towards them at a prodigious rate. It looked like some kind of enormous, bloated maggot, with curious protrusions here and there, almost like a gigantic, intergalactic caterpillar. But without the legs. Instead it had Plasma Torpedo Tubes, slung below the main body of the ship. They were beginning to glow red.

'Dave, fire up the Quantum Interstitial Drive and prepare to go to hyper speed!' said Harry.

'Will do, but we can't use the drive, not with the

space station so near. It's so big, its mass and energy banks interfere with the Q-Drive energy fields – basically, it won't work,' said Dave.

Gaggenow and the twins exchanged a look. 'Dave?' mouthed Gaggenow.

'Blast it!' said Harry, ignoring Gaggenow. 'How far away do we have to be before we can use it?'

'About where the Leptira are now,' said Dave. 'No, wait…not any more.'

Gaggenow began to whimper. The twins stared at the viewing screen, eyes wide and golden. Then they turned and stared at Harry. 'Do something!' they said.

'Yeah, all right, give me a chance! What about weapons systems – can we charge them up?' said Harry.

'Yes, Fusion Cannon can be ready in five point seven seconds, but you can't have the Q-Drive and the Fusion Cannon charged up at the same time.'

'What? Who designed this ship?'

'The Greys. And they don't like to fight,' said Dave. 'So which is it, Fusion Cannon or Q-Drive?'

'Will we be able to fire the Fusion Cannon before

those torpedoes… Whoa!'

The Leptira had fired. Two balls of bright blue energy flew from the torpedo tubes towards them.

'Shields up!' screamed Harry. 'Charge the Fusion Cannon! And take Evasive Action!'

Two more balls of bright blue energy, with tails of rushing green fire, sped towards them from the

belly of the *Raptor*. The *Fartface* swept back in the other direction, spilling the twins to the floor once more. Gaggenow, though, remained in his reflexive, defensive hump.

The torpedoes curved back in towards them, getting closer and closer.

'Tracking Torpedoes, I'm afraid,' said Dave.

'Yeah, I got that. Why aren't the shields up?' shouted Harry.

'Can't...do...everything at once, you know!' said Dave. Suddenly, a kind of transparent haze of energy enveloped the ship in a shimmering glow. 'There you go, shields up!'

'Just in time,' said Harry. 'Here they come! Dave, prepare to jink left...wait for it...wait for it...'

'Port...you mean port, it's port and starboard on a ship,' said Gaggenow, peering out from between his bony, knuckled fingers.

'Oh, shut up, you fish-faced kangaroo!' said Harry.

The Plasma Torpedoes were almost upon them. 'Now!!! Jink to port!' shouted Harry. The ship shifted to the left and for a moment it looked like the Plasma Torpedoes were going to fly harmlessly by, but at the last second they too shifted. They struck the starboard shields – there was a mighty flash of explosive power and the ship literally staggered. Lines of blue energy coruscated all over the shields…and dissipated. They had survived.

'Shields at eighty-seven per cent and recharging,' said Dave. 'But with Fusion Bank drain, recharging to one hundred per cent will take…twenty-three minutes…'

'Look, their Torpedo Tubes'

'are firing up again!' said the twins, pointing as one at the Leptira ship.

'How many more of those can we take before shields are down?' said Harry.

'Approximately seven such glancing blows, but a full-on strike…that would be bad!' said Dave.

'Can we hit their torpedoes with our Fusion Cannon? Or get close enough to hit their ship?' said Harry. 'Or maybe you could try a different dodging pattern, or…'

Dave interrupted him, 'Yes, that's great, Captain, although the Fusion Cannon will have no effect on the Plasma Torpedoes, but I can only do so much. We need to man these stations – here, here and here.' As Dave said this, three consoles lit up on the deck of the bridge.

'Weapons; Shields and Defensive Manoeuvres; and Sensor Comms,' said Dave.

'Right, got it! Alph, you're on Weapons; Bet, you're on Sensor Comms; Gaggs, get on Defence – I bet you'll be good at dodging stuff!' said Harry.

Without demur, Alph headed off, which was a surprise. Bet even said, 'Yes, sir!' which made Harry feel pretty good.

Gaggenow, though, said, 'I'm not getting involved. In fact, I'm off to my cabin – see you later!'

'Oh, Gaggenow,'

'how could you?' said the girls.

'Get back on that station, or we'll hand you off to the Leptira – it's you they want, not us!' said Harry angrily.

'All right, all right, I'll do it!' said Gaggenow, and he hopped over to the Shields and Defensive Manoeuvres console.

Bet chipped in: 'Sensors show the *Raptor* is about to fire another salvo…oh, and that there are about a thousand bio-readings…all Leptira, so many! Oh, and one… Well, that's odd!'

'What?' said Harry.

'Torpedoes away!!!' shrieked Bet, odd sensor readings forgotten. Immediately, Gaggenow tried to make a run for it.

'Get back on station, Gaggenow! NOW!' yelled Harry. 'Or this primitive Earth boy is going to kick your kangaroo butt!'

Gaggenow blinked and sat back down. 'Shields at eighty-eight per cent and climbing,' he said sheepishly.

'Alph, can you get a targeting lock on the *Raptor*?' said Harry.

'Umm…no, too far away, we'd need to be about twice as close as we are now,' she said.

'OK – Dave, head straight for those torpedoes!'

'What, are you mad?' said Alph.

'Right, that's it,' said Gaggenow, rising to his feet again.

'Wait, he's got a plan, we have to trust him!' said Bet.

Gaggenow paused, gripped with indecision. Harry got up, shoved Gaggenow back down, and then strapped him in. As he was doing this, he said, 'Dave, concentrate just on this, nothing else. At the last minute, we sheer off – those torps have got a wide turning circle, so it'll take 'em a while to get back on us. Meanwhile, we can get close enough to the Leptira to give 'em a broadside with the Fusion Cannon!'

'Yes!' said Alph and Bet, punching the air together. 'That's more like it!'

Gaggenow gulped.

The Wheelship hurtled toward the Plasma Torpedoes, as if to certain doom. The Plasma Torpedoes hurtled hungrily back at them.

'Dave, have you got this sorted?' said Harry.

'Shhh, I'm concentrating!' said Dave.

The torpedoes frothed with angry energy, arrowing towards them. The Wheelship raced to meet them…and at the last minute, ducked down beneath them! Over their heads, the torpedoes shot away.

'We did it!' yelled Gaggenow.

'Well done, Dave!' said Harry

'Fusion Cannon locked on target!' said Alph excitedly.

The *Fartface Banana Nose* banked away in front

of the vast Leptira battle cruiser. Behind them, the torpedoes streaked away, turning to follow them but in a wide, slow circle.

'FIRE!!!!!' said Harry. Four beams of bright yellow energy flashed out to hit the *Raptor's* forward shields. The Fusion Beams played across it, and then winked out.

'Bet, did that do any damage?' said Harry.

'Scanning… Umm… No, no, it didn't. Nothing at all; their shields…they've been recalibrated. Anti-Fusion Particle Shield…and they've put all their shield energy into their forward shields!'

'There is a zero per cent chance of damaging their shields, let alone penetrating them,' said Dave gloomily.

Harry blinked, disappointed.

'Leptira Torpedo Tubes charging again,' said Bet.

'We have to face facts,' said Gaggenow. 'We can't seem to hurt them. They'll have an almost unlimited supply of Plasma Torpedoes, they're bound to get us in the end!'

'Yeah, thanks for that, Gaggs,' said Harry.

'What's that?' said Bet. 'The Leaf Star – look!'

Behind them, a huge ship emerged from a docking bay on the resort station. It was the luxury liner, the SS *Bliss*. It heaved itself out, and then fired up its engines. Slowly, ever so slowly, it began to build up speed.

'Do you think they've come to help us?' said Harry, hopefully.

'Bah, of course not,' said Gaggenow. 'It's a pleasure ship – even fewer armaments than we've got! No, they'll be making a run for it, hoping to get to where they can hyper jump out of here. Don't want to hang around in case they get hit by a stray torpedo or something!'

Gaggenow stared at the liner wistfully.

'Plasma Torpedo impact imminent,' said Dave.

'But not to worry.' The two torpedoes crashed into the *Fartface Banana Nose*, but they'd taken so long to hit them, they'd been weakened quite a bit.

'Shields down to seventy-nine per cent but holding!' said Gaggenow.

'I'm sorry to bring this up, Harry, but the Fusion Banks are already being drained by maintaining the Hermetic Seal on the Hull breach in the cargo bay. What with the Fusion Cannon and the shields, we'll be getting through our power reserves rather more quickly than we would like!' warned Dave. 'A few more hits like that and we'll be toast!'

'INCOMING torpedoes!' said Dave.

This time, they managed to miss the first by charging at it head-on and jinking aside but were unable to fully avoid the other, and they took a big hit that rocked the ship from side to side.

'Shields at sixty per cent,' said Gaggenow. His feet drummed the floor, and his eyes flicked to the door.

'Gaggenow, even if you made it to the door where would you run to?' said an irritated Harry.

'Escape'

'Pods,' said the twins.

'We have Escape Pods?' said Harry.

'Oh, yes,' said Dave. 'One pod per crew member. The pods would head for the resort automatically but the Leptira would be able to pick them up, easy as pie.'

'Hah! But they might miss one whilst the ship and

the rest of us were still fighting, right, Gaggenow?'
said Harry, accusingly.

Gaggenow put on an expression of wounded
innocence. 'Oh, now, Captain, please, I never
thought such a thing, never!'

'How could you,' said the twins – for a moment
Harry thought they were on his side, but then they
continued:

'think such a thing?'

'Our Gaggenow wouldn't'

'abandon us like that!'

'Hah, you don't know the half of it,' said Harry,
irritated. They always took Gaggenow's side.

'Anyway, what are your orders, Captain?' said
Gaggenow, putting the onus cleverly back on Harry
before he could say more.

Harry's brow furrowed in thought. 'Could we
hide from them? Maybe behind the SS *Bliss*. I mean,
it's huge, they wouldn't be able to see us then. We
could tag along until we're far enough away from
the resort to make a jump.'

'Their sensors would still detect us easily. Plus,
they might just go through the *Bliss* to get to us,

blast it out of space at close range,' said Dave.

'Thousands of tourists'

'would die,' said the twins.

'Isn't there anything that could interfere with the Leptira sensors?' asked Harry.

'Well, actually…but no…that would be silly,' said Dave.

'What?' said Gaggenow, Harry and the twins all at the same time.

'The *Bliss*. Its Sub-hyper Propulsion System is a Positronic Annihilator Drive. The Leptira sensors cannot penetrate the engine backwash,' said Dave.

'So we could hide in the exhaust fumes of their engines, right, is that what you're saying?' said Harry excitedly.

'Well, yes,' said Gaggenow, 'for a few minutes, before the ship dissolves into positrons and is annihilated.'

'Aren't our shields positronic or something? What if we diverted all power to the forward shields, like the Leptira have done – would that protect us from the backwash of their engine drive?'

'Actually, yes,' said Dave. 'Shields would degrade…

umm…calculating…but quite slowly… We could survive there for approximately twenty-eight minutes.'

'Enough time for us to get far enough away to make a jump?' said Harry.

'Yes!' said Dave.

'That's it, that's our strategy! Dave, head for the *Bliss*,' said Harry.

'Yes, Captain!' said Dave.

'And Gaggenow, get ready to divert all power to forward shields. I'll tell you when,' said Harry.

'Hold on,' said Bet. 'There's an incoming message from the Leptira!'

A holo-monitor appeared in the air above them. A face formed… Harry recoiled at the sight of it. It was diamond-headed, not unlike the head of a mantis back on Earth, but big, big as a bear. Powerful blade-like mandibles hung down from either side of its mouth. Terrifying! And its eyes…that was the weird thing, its eyes were really very human-looking, which was rather unsettling.

'Try and keep it talking,'

'buy us some time,' whispered the twins. Harry nodded.

'GRARRAGHHHH!' went the face.

'A roar expressing the urgent desire for raw meat,' said the translator headset in Harry's ear.

'Aha!' continued the insect head in PanGal. 'There you are! Wait a minute, who the hell are you?'

'I know who I am, the question is who the hell are you?' said Harry.

'Don't bandy words with me, you mealworm! I'll rip out your heart and eat it in front of your eyes, you...'

'Actually, ripping out my heart would kill me instantly, so I wouldn't be able to see you eating it, so that would be pretty pointless,' said Harry defiantly.

Gaggenow put his hands over his head and sank deeper into his chair. The twins stared at Harry in amazement.

'Arrowargh!' said the mantis face, as it bobbed up and down in anger. 'I'll suck out your brains, I'll mash your liver and turn it into pâté, I'll mince you up and turn you into astro burgers, I'll…'

'Yeah, all right, I get it, but surely it's just common courtesy to tell me who you are before ripping me to bits and eating me?' said Harry. He was putting a brave face on it, but inside he was terrified.

The alien insect thing paused for a moment, as if pulling itself together. 'All right, then, I'll tell you. I am High Devourer Clypeus of the Leptira. And I am coming for you!' With that he leaned forward and clashed his mandibles together aggressively.

The twins and Gaggenow quailed in their seats. Harry, though, just stared back and frowned. 'What…I'm supposed to be scared or something, is that it?'

Clypeus the Leptira jerked his head back in

an expression that even Harry could recognise as astonishment. 'Don't you know how a High Devourer gets to be a High Devourer?' said Clypeus.

'Nope,' said Harry.

'Tell him, Gaggenow,' said Clypeus.

Gaggenow simply sank into his chair and whimpered. Clypeus raised his all too human eyes to heaven in a very man-like expression of exasperation. 'Bah, Ichthysupials, they're such cowards – Gaggenow especially. So, you really don't know?'

'No,' said Harry.

'Not from around here, eh? Well, it means I've personally killed and eaten two hundred and fifty people. At least! Scary or what?' he said, leaning forward again and gnashing his blade-like mandibles.

That actually was quite scary, but Harry wasn't going to let on. 'Well, I hope they gave you indigestion, you hideous freak monster!'

'What?! For that, your death will be slow and painful!!! I'll roast you over an open fire, I'll turn your skin into crackling, I'll parboil and then fry you alive, I'll…'

Another Leptira leaned into the frame and whispered something to Clypeus. Clypeus blinked a few times, in a strangely human way, as if getting a hold of himself.

'Anyway,' continued Clypeus, 'now you know who I am, who are you and what are you doing on that ship?'

'Why should I tell you?' said Harry.

Clypeus raised his eyes to heaven once more. 'Whatever,' he said. He leaned off screen, grabbed something that squealed, and came back holding someone in a clawed hand. He shoved its face forward to look into Harry's ship. It was a Grey, the one that'd been half decent to Harry, way back when all this started, the one that had clung to the table before being sucked into space. Somehow he'd survived, been plucked from space by the Leptira just in time. Though he looked in a bad way. He was bruised and scratched – and one arm was completely missing, bandaged up at the shoulder.

'Right, you little Grey rat,' said Clypeus. 'Who are this lot and what are they doing on your ship?'

The Grey blinked down at them, clearly terrified.

'Umm…Henry Greene, human adolescent, Sol Three, clone candidate; Alpha and Beta, Royal Yureshtian Clones, Inculcation Training completed, on Insertion Mission; and…err…an Ichthysupial, designation unknown, never seen him before.'

'You expect me to believe that you didn't know Gaggenow was on board? Hah, a likely story, you lying little Grey! I'll eat your other arm for that!' said Clypeus, reaching for it with a pincered claw.

'No, please,' whimpered the Grey, struggling pitifully like a tiny moth in the grasp of an enormous praying mantis.

'It's true. We didn't even know either,' said Harry quickly. 'Gaggenow was a stowaway, hiding in a scrap-metal cargo bay.'

Clypeus paused.

'Hmm, could be true, I suppose,' said Clypeus. 'Just like Gaggenow, come to think of it.' He put the Grey down, almost absent-mindedly. The little figure scuttled off, nodding at Harry gratefully along the way.

'So the poor little Greys didn't even know why we attacked, then? Hilarious!!!!' continued Clypeus. It put its head almost horizontally backward and made a strange staccato clicking noise. Leptira laughter.

Meanwhile, Harry mouthed to Bet, 'How long?' She held up a hand. Five minutes to the *Bliss*.

'Seems to me,' said Harry, 'you could have asked the Greys for Gaggenow. I'm sure they'd have given him up without all this fuss and fighting, but no, you had to go in there all guns blazing, like a bull in a china shop!'

Clypeus leaped to his feet – well, several of his insectoid feet, at any rate – and launched into another tirade of angry threats mixed with unusual recipes.

Harry smiled a small smile. Precious seconds were ticking by. Once again, another Leptira leaned into the frame to whisper in Clypeus's ear. Once again, Clypeus calmed himself, but not before he'd elbowed his colleague in the face and out of the way.

'Right, well... Anyway. Listen. Put Gaggenow, and all his luggage – *all* his luggage – in an Escape Pod and fire him into space. We'll pick him up. In return, we'll let you live,' announced Clypeus.

Gaggenow blinked up at Harry. 'Please, no, they'll eat me!' he said plaintively.

Harry thought for a moment. He'd really quite like to do that after what Gaggenow had done to him. But then again, these Leptira guys were pretty hardcore. They probably would eat Gaggenow. In some kind of lemon sauce or something. Would Harry want that on his conscience? But then again, he was a lying little... Hmm, choices, choices.

'Well, that sounds like an interesting deal, but how can we trust you?' said Harry. 'I mean, you could take Gaggs, and then still blast us out of space, right?'

'Actually, I was thinking of disabling your engines, and sending a bunch of marines over to capture you alive – never eaten human before. But I have to admit, you've been a bit trickier than I'd thought, hence the deal. But anyway, no, we wouldn't go back on our word, we're known for sticking to our deals, honest!' said Clypeus.

Harry looked over at Gaggenow and the twins. They shook their heads vigorously. Just as he thought, Clypeus and the others weren't to be trusted. So, even if he wanted to hand Gaggenow over, there was no guarantee the Leptira wouldn't eat them anyway.

'Another message incoming,' said Dave. 'From the *Bliss*.'

'Excuse me for a moment,' said Harry, actually glad of the chance to waste some more time.

'Bah, well, hurry it up, we haven't got all day, and I'm getting hungry. Actually, I'm always hungry,' said Clypeus.

A second holo-monitor appeared in the air – it was the captain of the *Bliss*, who, as it turned out, was another Ichthysupial like Gaggenow.

'What the blazes do you think you're doing, Captain Harry?' he said. 'Stay the hell away, you'll bring the Leptira down on us!'

'Captain Hib,' said Clypeus, 'it is I, High Devourer Clypeus of the Leptira Mantid Class battle cruiser *Raptor*! If you aid this Wheelship in any way, I'll personally eat you alive! Got it? Now, you're interrupting – get lost!'

'EEEEK!' said Captain Hib, and the monitor went dead. Bet nodded at Harry. They were close.

Harry shouted, 'Dave, put the *Bliss* between us and the *Raptor*, now!'

'Yes, Captain,' said Dave, and the *Fartface Banana Nose* shot forward.

'Hah!' said Clypeus. 'You think we haven't noticed you edging your way over there? You think you can hide behind the *Bliss*? You haven't got an Uxian Ice Ale's chance in the centre of the sun. We'll blast it to smithereens, and all that blood will be on your hands! Though the meat'll be in our bellies, hah, hah, hah! And then we'll come for you!'

As he was saying this, the *Fartface Banana Nose* glided neatly into position behind the *Bliss*, out of sight of the Leptira, though still within sensor range.

'The captain of the *Bliss* keeps signalling us to

stay away,' said Bet.

'Just ignore him!' said Harry. Off to their right – or rather starboard – Harry could see the fiery, yellow roar of the *Bliss's* engine exhausts. Harry stared at Gaggenow and jerked his head towards the rushing flames.

Gaggenow nodded. Dave whispered in Harry's ear, using the translator so that Clypeus couldn't hear, 'Gaggenow has diverted all power to forward shields. The ship is drifting slowly into the engine wash…'

And then they were in it, inside a coruscating blast of blazing energy, totally enveloped by it. Fire and flames washed over their screens in a great roaring rush, kept at bay by the thinnest of margins. The holo-monitor began to flicker fuzzily.

'What the…?' crackled Clypeus, his voice and face getting more and more blurry. 'What's happening, where have they gone? Sensors, give me a report wjboiwerkjh…kjafu…fizz…' Clypeus's voice suddenly winked out, along with the holo-monitor.

'Connection lost!' said Bet with a grin.

'It's working – I can hardly believe it,' said Alph.

Gaggenow smiled. 'Amazingly, it is!'

'Yeah, thanks for the vote of confidence, guys,' said Harry, though he was still grinning from ear to ear.

'You are a clever boy'

'for a commoner,' said the twins.

'Yes, good work, Harry,' said Gaggenow, 'though you couldn't have done it without my expert advice and seamless control of the shields, of course. But we're not out of it yet. We are, after all, inside the engine wash of an intergalactic spaceship, with only twenty minutes or so to live, and there's a Leptira battle cruiser waiting for us.'

'Shields at eighty per cent,' said Dave.

'Charge the Q-Drive, now!' said Harry.

'Yes, Captain.'

Alph and Bet frowned.

'How will we'

'know if it is'

'safe to use the'

'Q drive?' they said.

Gaggenow blinked. 'Good point,' he said. 'We can't be detected, it's true, but we can't detect anything either, so we'll have no idea how far we are from the space station.'

'Well, we'll just have to leave it to the last minute before we jump and take our chances,' said Harry.

'What, and just hope for the best? That's our plan, is it?' said Gaggenow.

'Yup. Unless you've got a better idea,' said Harry.

Everyone fell silent. The temperature on the bridge had got noticeably warmer, and was increasing all the time.

Harry began to sweat. 'Dave, is there anything we can do about this heat?'

'I'm afraid not,' said the computer. 'We are sitting right in the exhaust wash of an enormous space ship, after all; it really is a bit of a miracle that we haven't been shredded into atoms already, to be honest!'

'How hot is it going to get?'

'You will all pass out from heat exhaustion in about eleven minutes, give or take. You will all be dead – your blood will boil – in approximately eighteen minutes.'

'I thought we were going to get a good twenty-five minutes, Dave, that's what you said!'

'I'm sorry, you did ask how long the ship would survive, rather than yourselves. I am still a computer, you know, not a mind reader,' said Dave.

'Well, we'd better hope that we're far enough away from the Leaf Star to go into hyper space before our blood boils, then,' said Harry.

'Indeed,' said Gaggenow.

'Dave, do the hyper space Q-Drive jump in fifteen

minutes, no matter what. We'll be out of it but still alive, right?'

'Yes, just,' said Dave.

'Wait a minute,'

'I don't want to'

'faint from heat exhaustion,' said the twins.

'It's so'

'undignified!'

'Yeah, I know, but we have to maximise the time, right? If we jump too early, we'll have to charge the drive up all over again, and we'll be dead before it's ready again.'

Everyone was beginning to sweat profusely now as the heat rose to sauna-like levels.

'We have no choice, my Royal Tsarevnas,' said Gaggenow.

'Where would you like to jump to?' said Dave. 'Haddus Prime or Outpost 426?'

'Oh, Haddus Prime, of course,' said Gaggenow.

'Yes, it's got a proper'

'spaceport and everything,' said the twins.

If both Gaggenow and the twins wanted to go to Haddus Prime, that was reason enough to choose the Outpost, as far as Harry was concerned.

'The Outpost, Dave,' said Harry.

'Yes, Captain,' said the computer.

'But we don't want to go there,'

'it'll be some kind of horrible little'

'maintenance station or something,' said the twins.

'Indeed! What a dreadful prospect,' added Gaggenow.

'Well, the Leptira are still after us – they'll expect us to head for Haddus, so this will give us more time,' said Harry, clinching the argument.

The others fell silent. Soon they were all gasping for breath. Gaggenow slumped forward, the first to pass out. The twins followed suit a minute later, falling back in their seats in perfect harmony. Harry tried to hold on, but he couldn't breathe; his eyelids were like heavy blocks of lead, his mouth as dry as sand. Nausea racked his body but he was too weak to be sick. And then everything went black…

HARRY came to, his mouth as dry as dust. Gaggenow and the twins were still out of it, but the temperature had dropped to normal and they were alive and breathing.

'Where are we?' he said thickly.

'Outpost 426,' said Dave.

Harry looked out of the bridge observation window. Ahead, he could see a space station to which the *Fartface Banana Nose* was docked. It wasn't like the Leaf Star, though, it was tiny in comparison, not much bigger than the Wheelship. It was very simple in design, basically like an AAA battery hanging in space, with the Wheelship docked on one end and the other end pointing down to a big planet below. A big, dirty brown planet, with dirty green seas and patches of sprawling redness.

'Who lives here?' said Harry.

'Well, the Outpost is unmanned. It's a Hub station, a kind of automated "Consulate", from what I've learned from the Outpost AI. It's here to monitor the planet below.'

'The planet?'

'Yes, the locals call it "The Mound". The Hub calls it Tricrus 4.'

'Locals?' said Harry, still not really with it. He was so thirsty.

'Yeah, a race we call the Tricrusians. They've developed quite a sophisticated form of space travel, but they're not really that interested in other species and like to keep themselves to themselves. The Outpost has been put here so that the Hub can keep an eye on them. The Tricrusians put up with it, so that they can communicate with the Hub at any time, should they decide to do so. It's like an embassy but off-planet and completely automated.'

Beyond the planet, and up to the left, Harry could see a bright, blue light.

'Is that the sun? It's blue!' said Harry.

'Yup,' said Dave. 'It's a Class B main sequence star, and it's blue, cos it's really, really hot. Fortunately, we're quite a way from it. If we were as close as Earth is to your sun back home, we'd be burning up.'

'Any sign of the Leptira?' said Harry.

'No. Leptira battle cruisers are geared up for fighting; their Q-Drive is not so much of a priority. Takes them much longer to charge up their drives between jumps. They'll be stuck at the Leaf Star for quite a while yet.'

'Can we jump again?'

'As soon as we've refuelled and the fusion banks have been recharged, yes. Which I've started, by the way – thought you'd want to do that quickly, and the Outpost has plenty of fuel and supplies.'

'Good work, Dave,' said Harry as he staggered to his feet. 'Let me know when we're ready to jump, but for now, I need water.'

Harry headed for the door, weaving like a drunken man. Behind him, Gaggenow and the twins slept on.

He found one of the water coolers in a nearby corridor, and drank his fill. That made him feel a lot better. He looked up, eyes finally coming back into focus. Harry was opposite Gaggenow's 'Luxury Guest Room'.

He narrowed his eyes in thought. 'Dave,' he said, 'open Gaggenow's room.'

'Yes, Captain,' said Dave, and the door swished open. Harry marched in. 'Let me know when Gaggenow comes round, Dave.'

'Right, got it,' said the computer.

Harry began to search through Gaggenow's stuff. Clypeus had wanted Gaggenow handed over, 'and *all* his luggage'. Maybe it wasn't really Gaggenow everyone was after, but something he had. Something he'd stolen.

Gaggenow didn't have much stuff – hardly surprising, as he'd been a stowaway. Just a few clothes and his holo-harness – broken now – plus various bits and pieces. And then…a sports bag! A more earthly thing you could not get; obviously from the time Gaggenow had been hiding out there. What was that doing here? Harry unzipped it. Inside was a typical Earth supermarket plastic bag! And inside that, a large, black velvet box. And inside that… Harry's jaw dropped. An enormous jewel, about the size of a tennis ball, maybe a little bigger, and as heavy as lead. In essence, it was the biggest diamond you could ever imagine – except when you held it up to the light, you could see what looked like tiny pinpricks of light in lots of different colours. As if it held an entire universe of stars inside. Harry put it back in the bag and sighed. It was worse than he'd thought. Much worse.

But he'd kind of expected it, really. He was fairly sure he'd seen it before. In that photo the Grey captain had of their holiday on Hub Prime, the photo of the Imperial Regalia, the crown jewels. With Gaggenow hanging around in the background… And also in that issue of the *Supernova*.

'Dave, did you see that?' said Harry.

No reply. 'Dave? Are you there?'

'What? Oh, yes, Harry, sorry, I was just verifying data. I mean…I can hardly believe it, and I'm a computer! But yes. It is. I'm afraid.'

'The crown jewel? From Hub Prime?' said Harry.

'Yes. The Crown Starheart,' said Dave, almost reverently.

'What is it, anyway?'

'Well, it's the galaxy's largest known Starheart, which is a kind of diamond, created in the heart of a supernova. One of the rarest things in the galaxy…'

'Wow!' said Harry. 'It must be worth…'

'A fortune. More than that, actually – a planet! A solar system, even,' said Dave. 'The Crown Starheart is not just the largest in the known galaxy, it's also the main part of the Crown…the Imperator's Crown.'

'Imperator?' said Harry.

'Yes, the Imperator Ultimata. The supreme ruler of the Hub. The Galactic Overlord who sits on the Galactic Throne, in the Palace of Palaces, on Hub Prime, the capital, a huge artificial planet that orbits the black hole at the centre of the galaxy. The most powerful being in the galaxy, possibly the universe….'

Harry blanched. Oh dear. What had he got himself into? He'd thought Gaggenow was just a two-bit fraudster on the run, but, actually he was probably one of the most wanted people in the universe. No wonder the Leptira were after them! And the reward… Harry was surprised it wasn't more, but that kind of made sense. The Imperator wouldn't want the real truth to get out; it'd make him look like a fool. But how had Gaggenow pulled that off? He seemed such an obvious liar and trickster. Hah, this must have been the greatest scam of his life!

So that's why it seemed like the entire galaxy was after a fourteen-year-old boy from Croydon, Harry thought to himself.

He shook his head and sighed again. What a pickle. There had to be a way out of this, though, so he could get home to Earth without being pursued by all the bounty hunters in the entire galaxy, not to mention the Galactic Police.

'Couldn't we just fly to the nearest GalPol Station and hand it in?' said Harry.

'Possibly,' said Dave. 'But it is a strategy fraught with risk. It would be a terrible temptation to any who saw it, police or not. There are many enemies of the Hub who would pay hugely for it. Also, there is no guarantee that you wouldn't simply be hauled off yourself, never to be seen again. They'll want to keep its loss, even if returned, well under wraps. It's bound to make them look bad, and if they want to keep it for themselves – well, they're not going to let you live so you can blab about it.'

'But we can't lug it around with us, we'll be hunted down like rats, wherever we go!' said Harry.

'Indeed. You'll just have to think of a way to get rid of it cleverly. Maybe do a deal with the Imperator – actually, no one gets to speak to him. Hmm, I guess maybe you could talk to one of his top blokes, like the Vizier Vexillarius or someone,' said Dave.

'Oh sure, how am I going to do that then? I can't just ring him up, can I? Yo, Vexillarius old son, how you doing, mate?' said Harry.

'No, the title is Vizier Vexillarius, his actual name is Plodington Plods,' said Dave.

'Oh, come on, you're having a laugh,' said Harry.

'No, Plodington Plods. Vizier. One of the most powerful people in the galaxy.'

'Hah! Plodington Plods, what a name!' Harry said, chuckling. Then he had another idea. 'What if we just handed this over to Clypeus? Or maybe sold it to him? Would they leave us alone then?'

'I think not. They won't just be wanting the Starheart, they'll be wanting all the people involved. To cover it up, but for interrogation too, I would think. Thorough interrogation. I reckon there's no way Gaggenow could have taken that on his own, he'll have had inside help. And they'll want to find out who, and Clypeus will want every credit of that reward.'

'I see...' said Harry, frowning miserably. 'This is terrible – that fish-faced kangaroo, he's going to get us all killed!'

'Actually, he's just woken up and is on his way. He is stopping for a drink.'

'Right, I'm out of here and I'm taking the Starheart with me!' said Harry, stuffing it up his T-shirt. Out the room he sped, and down the corridor. He turned a corner – to see Gaggenow heading towards him.

'Are you all right, young man?' said Gaggenow.

'And what's that bulge…?' Harry just ignored him and flew right on past. Gaggenow frowned. 'No, it couldn't be…' he muttered to himself. 'Could it?'

And with that he began to run too, heading for his room, feet flopping against the floor like flippers. Meanwhile, Harry swept into his cabin. 'Dave, seal that door! Don't let anyone in, no matter what they say or do, especially Gaggenow. Got that?'

'Yes, Captain, the door is sealed. You'd need a Heavy LazGun to cut through it.'

'Great, thanks,' said Harry, stuffing the Starheart into an old blanket and shoving it under the bed. 'After all we've been through, I'm totally knackered. I need some sleep.'

With that, he lay down on the bed. Seconds later, he was asleep.

HARRY woke suddenly, unable to move his hands and legs. What the…?! He looked around. He was inside a large, coffin-shaped tube, strapped into some kind of cushioned bunk. He couldn't move. There was a heavy, transparent lid open in front of him. How had he got here?

'Dave, what's going on?' he shouted.

A voice sounded from an intercom by his head: 'Computer offline. Running Level Five Maintenance, All Systems Scan, Defrag, Virus Checker, Quantum Stabiliser and Logical Dichotomy Resolution Routines. Dave apologises, and says he will be back online in thirty-five minutes.'

Then Gaggenow's face appeared, standing over him. Harry stared up at him in shock.

'Thought you'd keep the Starheart for yourself, eh?' Gaggenow said, scowling down at him. 'Well, this time I'm going to get rid of you once and for all, meddling monkey boy!'

'No way, I was going to find a way to give the thing back, so that they'd leave us alone, so we could be free – all of us, I wasn't going to keep it!' said Harry, straining at his bonds.

'Oh, please, don't try to kid a kidder. Anyway, it's too late for that,' said Gaggenow. He was reaching for the door, ready to seal Harry in whatever he was in.

'You're going to kill me, aren't you?' said Harry, struggling even harder at the straps that bound him, but to little effect.

'What? No, no, dear boy, of course not,' said Gaggenow. 'It's just that it'll all be so much easier with you out of the way. The girls respond so well to flattery, and the whole steward/Tsarevna thing is such an excellent cover. And with this ship…well, you had to go, sorry.'

Gaggenow started closing the door again. Harry thought furiously. He had to buy time.

'How'd you get in my room, anyway?' he said.

Gaggenow paused. 'Ah, now that was really clever of me, really it was! You thought you were safe in your cabin, what with Dave keeping the door sealed, didn't you? Well, I initiated a Maintenance Scan – knocked Dave off the mainframe for a while, allowed me an opportunity to programme the door to open. Crept in, applied a sedative, bang, out you go. Starheart? Under the bed! Typical ape, no imagination. And bingo, here you are! Goodbye; nice knowing you, Harry!' And with that, he began to close the door again.

'Wait, where am I? What is this thing you've got me in?' said Harry.

Gaggenow paused again. 'It's an Escape Pod, you

needn't worry – well, in the sense that you won't die. I'm going to maroon you on the planet below. They're civilised enough and the atmosphere is near Earth normal. You'll be fine.'

Harry glared at him. 'You fish-faced freak!' he said. 'If I ever get out of this, I'll find you, just you wait and see, I'll find you!'

'Of course you will,' said Gaggenow. 'Earth boy marooned on the wrong side of the galaxy without a ship will find the Great Gaggenow. Hah, the Imperator's Guardians couldn't find me! GalPol couldn't find me! How are you going to?'

'That Clypeus geezer, he found you – I outwitted him for a start!'

Gaggenow frowned at that.

'Bah,' he said. 'Whatever. I've left you with a pack and a few supplies, some credits, and uploaded Tricrusian to your translator. You'll be fine. Goodbye!' And he slammed the door shut.

The intercom spoke in his ear. 'Welcome to your Survivor 2000 Personal Escape Pod. I will be your Assistant AI for your journey. You may call me Pod 14. Launch protocols have begun. This pod will be fired into space in approximately three minutes and counting.'

'Pod 14, abort launch!' said Harry, desperately.

'Launch cannot be aborted. Safety override enacted.'

Harry stared around wildly, but what could he do? He wracked his brains but…nothing, he could think of nothing.

'Two minutes and counting…'

Harry shut his eyes and screamed, 'Noooooooooooo!'

Suddenly, there was a loud hiss and the door began to open. 'Warning, warning, Escape Pod door open!' said the pod computer.

Harry opened his eyes. It was Bet! She'd come to save him, thank God!

'Get me out of here!' shouted Harry.

Bet shook her head. 'Can't,' she said.

Harry stared at her in astonished horror. 'The straps, undo the straps,' pleaded Harry.

'No, it's Gaggenow, we… I can't…' she spluttered incoherently. Tears welled up in her golden eyes. She leaned down and put something into the pod.

A siren began to blare, and a red warning light to flash.

'Warning, Airlock Decompression imminent!' screamed the intercom in his ear. 'Seal pod doors and vacate hold immediately!'

Bet said something, but Harry couldn't hear her over the sound of the siren. She leaned down and spoke, her lips lightly brushing his ear.

'It's a tracker, amongst other things. With it you can find the ship. And us – me,' she said.

Harry nodded his thanks. Her face was close to his, very close. He could see a tear rolling down her cheek – it was the same colour as her eyes. It looked like liquid gold.

'I'm so sorry,' she said, and she kissed him. Fiercely. Before he could say a word, she'd turned away and slammed the pod door shut without a second look. She was gone.

'Forty-five seconds to pod launch and counting.'

Harry stared out of the pod, trying to understand what had just happened, but he couldn't really get his head round it. Girls! They just didn't make sense sometimes. And even worse, after all he'd been through he was just going to be fired out into space? This couldn't be happening!

'Escape Tube Airlock open,' said Pod 14.

'Pod 14! Stop it, stop it now, stop the launch!' Harry shrieked desperately.

'Unable to comply. Three, two, one, LAUNCH!'

Suddenly Harry was wrenched back into his harness as the Escape Pod shot forward like a bolt from a crossbow. All Harry could see was a metal wall flying past as the pod was fired down some kind of tube that kept twisting and turning along the way. It was a bit like one of those tubular water slides in aqua parks back home on earth. Except that he wasn't going to land in a nice, warm pool with lots of other laughing children having fun. Oh no, he was going to be fired out into the cold, empty wastelands of space instead.

He shot out into endless night. All he could see were the stars, a sea of stars. Then the *Fartface Banana Nose* hove into view – he was flying past it. It was a huge wheel of gleaming silver steel, with silver spokes attached to a circular hub at the centre, where the bridge and the galley were housed. Staterooms and cabins were on the outer ring. Harry noticed movement on board. There! It was Gaggenow, on the bridge, sitting in the captain's chair. Gaggenow waved at him languidly, and then gave him one final, mocking salute. Harry ground his teeth in anger.

Pod 14 began to shoot up and over the Wheelship, across the face of the Observation Deck on top of the central hub. Now Harry could see the twins through the window! Incredibly, it looked like they were having an argument, though obviously he couldn't hear a word. But he could see plenty. Alph was shoving a finger in Bet's face and shouting at her. Bet had her head in her hands, and was sobbing.

'Hah!' said Harry to himself. 'I bet Alph is having a go at her for giving me that tracking device.' He sighed. *Boy, she must really hate me*, he thought.

And then they were gone…

He shot past the ship and out into space. There was nothing but stars ahead. He wasn't heading to the planet at all – Gaggenow had lied! Harry's heart began to race as it filled with fear. A terrible fear, one he had never felt before; he was hurtling into emptiness and he had no control over it, no say, no way to fight back. Was this how he would die, flying through space to nowhere? Would the oxygen run out, suffocating him? He hoped so – that would be better than starving to death, trapped, unable to move, forever alone in the unending black.

Then the pod seemed to dip forward, and a large, dirty brown mass began to creep into view.

'Commencing approach to Tricrus 4,' said Pod 14.

Harry heaved a sigh of relief. Soon the planet filled his vision entirely, a swirl of brown, green and red. Harry stared at it in horrified fascination. He wasn't going to die in space, but still…what was down there? Now it was the fear of the unknown that filled his heart – but tinged with a certain excitement. It was better than sitting in detention back at school, that was for sure. On the other hand, it was a tad more dangerous...

The planet grew in size. Harry could see clouds in the air. Some of them had a weird greenish tinge.

'Calculating optimal atmospheric entry trajectory,' said Pod 14. A few seconds passed.

'Atmospheric entry in... Three, two, one, now!'

There was a sudden impact and the pod began to shake and rattle so hard that Harry thought his teeth were coming loose. Things started to heat up, fast. Outside, all he could see was fire, completely enveloping the pod. He began to sweat profusely – it seemed like something had gone wrong. The pod was disintegrating and he was going to get burned up in the atmosphere!

'AAAARRRRRRRRGHHHHH!' he screamed.

And then...sudden stillness. Total silence. He was high up in the air – the horizon a wide arc under a yellowing sky over a dirty-brown world, criss-crossed with wisps of green. White clouds, smudged with a greenish hue, floated serenely by.

'Deploying chute,' said Pod 14. There was a cracking sound, a sudden lurch and then they were drifting down. The ground began to race up to meet him, a dirty muddy ground, coming up way too fast.

'We're coming in too fast, we're going to crash!' Harry said in a panicky voice.

'Please, sir, remain calm,' said Pod 14.

'Remain calm? We're going to...' wailed Harry.

'Extending Landing Gear,' interrupted Pod 14, 'and initiating controlled descent protocols.'

Harry puffed out his cheeks in relief. Whatever that meant, it sounded good! The pod shuddered as some kind of engine roared into life, and then it began a slow descent.

Daintily, it touched the ground, a perfect landing.

'Initiating Distress Beacon. We hope you have enjoyed your Survivor 2000 experience. For your information, the primary native species of this planet call it "The Mound". Pod 14 program complete. Computer shut down. Welcome to the Mound.'

The straps holding Harry down popped open, and so did the door. All Harry had to do was to step out of the pod, and he would be on the surface of another planet...

HARRY stood upright in the Escape Pod, a little scared to step out into the unknown. He breathed in the air. It had a kind of earthy smell, with a metallic tang underneath, and a hint of boiled cabbage and eggs. Rather unpleasant, really. Ahead, he could see an expanse of brown mud, then some tall grass-covered mounds. Except that the grass wasn't green, but a dark, ruddy red in colour. And beyond that – a sort of forest, perhaps? The trees weren't very tall – more like thick round stumps, but each stump had a kind of big, wide, rusty red hat on it, just like the sort of thing medieval Chinese peasants used to wear back home on Earth.

In the distance, a mountain of brown rose up into the yellow sky, topped with what could only be green snow. Off to the left, Harry could see a kind of pool, into which ran a waterfall. Quite Earth-like…

except that the water was a bright emerald green. And something else…oh yes, nothing grew around the pool, or the waterfall, or the river that ran from the pool. Odd.

Harry took a tentative step forward…onto thick, sludgy mud. His foot sank into it, right up to his ankles. And then he felt it. Crushing down on him.

The gravity.

His body felt as heavy as lead; his lungs had to work twice as hard to breathe. He couldn't stand for long, his legs were already shaking, just holding him upright. He had to sit down, now. In the mud. Even that was hard. He flopped onto his back and lay

there for a moment, just trying to breathe, shielding his eyes from the bright blue sun. It was a tiny dot in the sky, but it glared down at him like an angry eye.

Yes, the atmosphere was breathable, but that wretch Gaggenow hadn't mentioned the gravity! It felt like twice that of Earth. How was he going to stand this?

Harry groaned. He hauled himself over to the Pod, reached in and dragged out the device Bet had put in there, and the backpack Gaggenow had left. The backpack was called a 'Survivor 2000 Packhorse' according to the label. It felt soooo heavy. It took him a while just to get his gear out, let alone put Bet's device into the pack and strap it all to his back. Harry looked around. He couldn't see anything moving or alive. Which was just as well. What if some kind of predator came along?

He had to do something, though. He looked over at the mounds. At least he could lean up against them. Harry tried to get up, but the effort it took just to stand left him panting for breath, let alone walking. So he dropped down to all fours. He couldn't even maintain that for long, and soon he was face down in the mud, crawling to the mound. Finally, after what seemed like an age of suffering and pain, he reached one of the mounds. It took his final reserves of energy just to prop himself up against it. He was covered in mud and drenched in sweat. Rivulets ran down his legs and arms, so that he looked like some kind of striped ape.

As he lay there, getting his breath back, he noticed that what he'd thought was grass growing on the mound really wasn't very grassy. It was much more like…well, fur. And the mound itself didn't seem to be of earth or mud – rather it was quite solid and smooth, beneath the fur. Some kind of rock, perhaps?

Anyway, it was time to take stock, find out what he had to hand. He reached inside his 'Packhorse' and found several round containers, a kind of thermo-flask with a mirrored panel on it, a cylindrical object that he took to be a torch, and three rectangular plastic chips, as well as the device Bet had given him. He examined the chips. They were inlaid with curious strands of some kind of metal, and covered in what he could now recognise to be numbers, in PanGal. He suspected they were one thousand Galactic Credit chips. Not exactly generous, but not too miserly either. Not that there was anywhere to spend them, mind you.

The flask was full of liquid. He sniffed it. Odourless. Took a swig…. Water. He gulped greedily. Just then a light winked on the flask, and a little voice piped up, 'Hi, I'm your personal Survivor 2000 HydroPal!' It was a kind of soothing girl's voice, sort of cutesy, like the voice that Marilyn Monroe used to put on in those old-time films back home on Earth.

'My solar collector energy panel has detected a good source of sunlight – would you like me to energise my Atmospheric Distillers for you, sweetie?'

Harry blinked at it in astonishment. 'Atmospheric…what?' he said.

'Atmospheric Distillers, dearie. I have a wonderful pair of solar-powered Distillers, you know. So long as there's sunlight, and the right kind of atmosphere, I can make water for you to drink, for ever and ever!'

'Awesome!' said Harry. 'Yes, please!' At least water wasn't going to be a problem.

Then he reached into his backpack and pulled

out one of the jars. It took some effort to open it in this gravity, but he managed it. His heart sank as the smell of what was inside wafted up to his nostrils. Nutrit Porridge. He sighed and checked the rest – yup, all porridge. Still, he wouldn't starve. Well, not for…hmm, about a week if he rationed it out. That wasn't good.

Then he pulled out the torch. One end had a lamp, the other a button. Down one side there was a silvery mirror – the torch must be solar-powered as well. He hit the button. Suddenly, it spoke too!

'Hello, sir!' it said in a deep soldierly voice, like a US Marine back on Earth. 'I am your Survivor 2000 Multi-Knife! Give me an order, sir!'

'Umm…what kind of thing can you do?' said Harry, staring at it.

'I'm as tough as nails, sir! I've got three modes: Recon, Combat and Survival!'

'Wow, cool!' said Harry. 'How do I activate you?'

'Just call me Sergeant and give me some orders.'

'OK…umm…Sergeant. Recon Mode!' said Harry.

'Yes, sir! Going Recon!' said the Sergeant. The torch end winked into life, a nice powerful beam of light. The handle shifted, and a display appeared on one side. A readout – calibrated for Earth English (grudgingly, Harry thanked Gaggenow for that) – showing distances in metres.

'Motion detector,' said the Sergeant. 'Will detect hostiles in a 500 metre radius – well, friendlies too, but as my daddy always said, "Treat 'em all as hostiles until they ain't any more."'

'Your daddy?'

'Yeah, well, I call him my daddy. He was a programmer, really.'

'Right… Anyway, what about Combat Mode?' said Harry.

'OK, I can't right now, the way you're holding me. Point me away from your body…that's it… Combat Mode! Let's kick butt!'

Suddenly, a long, slightly curved, three-foot blade leaped forth from the end of the Multi-Knife. The

blade was of matt black steel, and as sharp as anything. The rest of it moulded itself into a two-handed grip. Harry grinned in delight. A sword, a hi-tech samurai-style sword! How cool was that? Mind you, in this gravity, it would be almost impossible for him to actually use it for long.

'OK, Sergeant, let's go into Survival Mode,' said Harry.

'Yessir!'

The blade snapped back into the main body, and then out again, but this time as a three-inch knife. The rest of it kind of folded itself inside out, revealing several useful little metal tools – a saw, a screwdriver, a gouger and so on. Even a small blowtorch for starting fires and heating things. Essentially, a kind of Swiss Army knife. Or Galactic Army knife, more like.

Harry turned to the device Bet had given him. It looked like a slim touchscreen computer, about the size of a book. He touched it and it came to life.

The words faded, to be replaced with a small star map of this area of the galaxy, showing Haddus and Tricrus and a couple of other nearby stars, MikMak and Pryzl. Tricrus was flashing red. A message box said 'Tracking Beacon located at Outpost 426, Tricrus.'

Harry looked up at the sky. They were still up there somewhere. He sighed. So near, yet so far. How could they do this to him? Well, he'd show them! He'd survive this, find a way to get off this planet, track them down and then...oh, then there'd be a reckoning!

He looked back at the GalNav Tracker. He touched the flashing Tricrus star symbol with a finger. Another screen popped up, showing a close-up of the planet and some information on its flora and fauna.

Tricrus 4 (Native name 'The Mound')

The Mound is a sparsely populated planet because of its soil, which is a thick mud high in metals and other toxic elements, making it very hard for complex plant and animal life to exist. Its rivers, lakes and seas, however, are choked with a kind of green algae. This algae is enough to sustain certain life forms including the Red Platus, the Green Platus and thus the Terrible Eater.

Red Platus

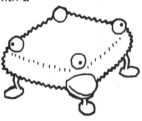

The Red Platus is flat and square, with a single duck-like bill at one corner, used for filtering the algae out of the water. Eyes on top and at each corner allow the Platus to keep a look out for predators at all times. The body rests on four squat legs, barely an inch or two in height. Its red fur is actually photosynthetic and can create sugars in the bright, powerful sunlight of the Mound, just like the leaves on a plant.

Green Platus

The Green Platus is much the same, except that it has developed a symbiotic relationship with the green algae. Algae is incorporated into the skin cells of the Platus, turning the skin green.

The Terrible Eater

The Eater is a carnivorous beast that feeds on the Red and Green Platus (or anything else it can get). Basically, it's a huge mouth and stomach, set atop four short but massive legs. It has an enormous muscular tongue, covered in a thick, sticky saliva, which it uses to suck up its prey. It hunts only at night.

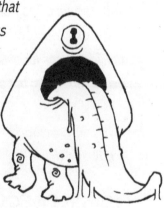

Intelligent Life

The Tricrusians are squat, three-legged beings. From this sturdy tripod springs a thick barrel torso with two powerful arms, ending in three-fingered hands. The head, atop a thick neck, is quite humanoid, similar to the Greys of Canus Prime, the blue-skinned, golden-eyed Yureshtians, the Medusans, the Fays, the Ragglers and the rest of the humanoids. Little is known about them. The mud makes for an excellent source of various rare metals and elements. The Hub is currently negotiating with the Tricrusians for mining and extraction rights, but to little avail.

This entry compiled by: Professor Verdlop Mimmlesip, Professor of Xenothropology, University of Fornax.

Harry put the GalNav down. Marooned on the weirdest planet in the galaxy. Typical. The sun was going down, slowly drifting to the horizon across the yellow sky. It would be night soon. He looked over at the lake.

'Sergeant!' he said.

'Yessir,' said the Multi-Knife.

'Go Recon, but don't use the torch beam – save energy. I'm going to need that motion detector on at all times,' said Harry.

'Yes, sir!' said the Sergeant.

Harry checked the detector. No signs of life around the lake and waterfall. That was good. But night was coming, and that's when the Terrible Eaters hunted. He really didn't want to meet one of those. Anyway, he'd have to sleep here, nothing else for it. His Survivor 2000 Packhorse bag could be opened out to double as a thermal blanket, so he'd be warm enough. Maybe tomorrow he'd have acclimatised to the gravity enough to get moving. He had to find some Tricrusians – it was his only chance to get off this planet. Assuming they were friendly…

21 NIGHT TERRORS

HARRY woke with a start in the night. Something had been nagging at his brain. But he didn't have time to think about that.

'Motion detected,' hissed the sergeant. '233 metres, heading parallel to this position, sir!'

Harry could hear rustling noises from the lake area. Suddenly, there was a cacophony of hooting and shrilling and splashing, followed by a horrible slithering sound that frightened the hell out of Harry. Was that a shape, in the starlight, over by the lakeshore, a lumbering, massive shape, thrashing around in the dark? And the noise! It went on and on, a kind of horrible trumpeted screaming as if from a hundred-voiced choir of the damned. Scores of little red dots flashed up on his motion detector, buzzing around like flies.

Harry sank back into the mound, terrified.

'Combat mode, sir?' said the sergeant.

'No!' hissed Harry. 'And be quiet!' He stared into the night, heart thudding in his chest. After a few minutes, the sounds began to die down, and everything faded into silence. Harry stared at the motion detector. A single red dot flashed. It began to move. Slowly.

It was coming towards the mounds! Harry watched with mounting horror as the little dot crept closer and closer. Slowly. Implacably.

He tried to sink further back into the mound, pushing himself against it. The mound gave a little: not much, but Harry was pushing without thinking. Something in the mound gave suddenly, with a sharp, loud crack. The red dot stopped moving.

Harry froze in fear, hardly able to breathe, hunter and prey both as still and as silent as the night itself. And then the dot began moving again – directly towards him!

Harry's mind raced. What could he do? Get up and run? In this gravity, in the dark? Not an option. He gripped the multi-knife in his hand. Combat Mode would be the last resort... For now, though

– quiet and silent, and hope whatever it was moved on by.

Harry heard something. There, again! It was a slow rhythmic drumming. A kind of heavy, slapping, 'wap-a-dup-dup' for a second or two. And then silence. Then another 'wap-a-dup-dup'. Then silence for a few more seconds. Then the noise again. It was like something heavy being drummed against the mud. And again…the sound was getting louder and closer all the time.

The motion detector showed the dot was fifty metres away. Suddenly he heard a kind of gasping noise, and it began to head towards him more quickly. The strange drumming sound grew faster, more insistent!

The light, the red dot, flashing in the night: it was giving his position away! Quickly Harry shut it off. A strange hiss came from the dark, like a shallow, rattling moan. And then silence, total silence. Except for Harry's heart beating in his chest, like the soundtrack of a rock video. Harry tried to calm his heart, fearful that the thing – whatever it was – would be able to hear.

Silence reigned.

And then… 'Wap-a-dup-dup.' Silence. 'Wap-a-dup-dup' – drawing near. Now Harry could make out another sound, in the intervals between moves. A wet slithering followed by a strange 'phut!' sound.

It made Harry think of snakes and lizards, tasting the air with their tongues. He shuddered, the fear rising inside him. And then…wafting over him, the smell of it, whatever it was. A kind of rancid odour of decay, like the smell of a rotting, stagnant pond.

And now, the stars on the horizon, they were blocked out by something wide and massive. It was nearly upon him! Harry felt a surge of utter terror mushrooming up inside him – he couldn't take it, he had to know what was there! He pointed his multi-knife and switched on the torch beam.

A bright white light split the night, shining right onto…an enormous pyramid-shaped head, with a single huge eye, over a cavernous, toothless mouth, out of which writhed a vile, blood-coloured tongue of immense size, like a gigantic tentacle.

Harry screamed, a scream of pure, primordial terror.

The Terrible Eater – for that is what it was – reared back from the light, and warbled a fluting cry of its own. Its single eye folded in on itself – there were no eyelids – and its tongue wrapped protectively around its head.

Harry, terrified, screamed, 'Combat Mode!' at the top of his voice. The blade leaped forth – and the torch winked out, plunging Harry into total darkness. Adrenaline coursing through his body, he raised the sword and brought it down instinctively, blindly, with all his power and strength. It struck something soft and spongy, cutting straight through it to bury itself in the muddy ground.

There was an awful squealing sound, like a hundred dying pigs. Nearby, something heavy splashed into the mud. The squealing continued but Harry couldn't see a thing. He could hear something loping away though, as fast as it could go, its four massive pillar-like legs drumming the ground in a frenzy, warbling in pain and fear as it went.

Harry was panting heavily; the effort of wielding the sword in this gravity had taken nearly all his strength. Close by, something was writhing in the mud...

Harry, his heart in his mouth, said, 'Sergeant, go Recon.' Suddenly the blade whipped back – which made Harry fall onto his knees, as he'd been leaning on it – and the torch beam came on. Harry shone it in the direction of the writhing... What he saw made him lurch back in disgust and horror! It was the tongue, the Terrible Eater's tongue – huge, long, snake-like, and still moving in squirmy spasms. Harry stared at it in horrified fascination. Gradually, the twitching began to die down, until at last it stopped.

It was over.

22 EGGS NIHILO

HARRY opened his eyes, a thought forming at the back of his brain. But there were more important things to worry about and he sat bolt upright, half expecting a writhing, bloody tongue to be wrapped around him, dragging him into an enormous maw of reeking foulness. But no, that was the last vestige of a nightmare. No, wait, it hadn't been a nightmare, had it?

He looked up – and had to shield his eyes. The bright blue sun was rising up over the horizon, bathing the land in a bluish glow. Emerald clouds and a golden yellow sky, and everywhere a diamond blue light played across the mud, chasing the night away. It was really quite beautiful. Harry began to get to his feet. He heaved himself up the side of the mound – but his hopes of acclimatisation were just that – hopes. It took all his energy just to stand.

He leaned back against the tall mound, gasping for breath, and gazed out at the sunrise.

Then the green clouds, the waterfall and the lake began to glitter and sparkle, as if thousands of fireflies swam in their waters, or flew in the clouds. The effect was mesmerising. He guessed it was the green algae that lived in the water, responding to the first rays of light of the day with some kind of photo-luminescence.

Everywhere, a soft, blue-tinged mist rose off the mud, as the sun heated the ground. Behind him, he heard a gentle thudding hiss. And then another. He looked over at the red-hatted forest of stumps. Some of the 'hats' were rising gently into the air, floating up on the warm thermals of the early morning. Some unseen biological mechanism was firing them up to soar on the warming air. They went up and up and up...when suddenly they burst into a cloud of red spores, glittering in the sunlight like a firework, there to ride the high winds in search of new lands to pollinate.

Sunrise was truly beautiful on Tricrus. But then a great wash of melancholy washed over Harry. It was beautiful, but last night he'd been almost eaten. And he could barely walk, and he was alone, so alone. Beautiful, deadly, empty…

He put his hands into his pockets and sighed, watching the sunrise.

His fingers curled automatically around his mobile phone, still in a pocket on the side of his trousers. He took it out and turned it on. His inbox was mostly full of old texts from his mum. He read through them, eyes filling with tears. Most were messages like 'where are you?' (hah, if only she

knew!) and 'get home now!' or 'school phoned, what have you done this time?' and so on, but none of that seemed to matter any more. He would do anything to get a text from her now, no matter what it said.

He began a reply to one of her texts, though he knew she'd never get it. And he typed it out properly, not using text speak, as he knew his mum hated that. And anyway, it wasn't as if he was in a hurry or anything. He wrote, 'It's amazing, the universe. Huge. And when you get out into it, all the stupid stuff doesn't seem to matter any more. When you're amongst all those stars, and worlds, and beings, you can finally see what's important. Anyway. I wish you could've seen me fighting the Leptira! It was grand, Mum, really grand. Love you. And goodbye. Harry. xxx'

Harry looked back up at the sky. Suddenly, the thought that had been nagging at the back of his brain since he'd got here bubbled up to the surface – the Wagglestaff Corporation! They made the GalNav Tracker, right. But they also owned that *Supernova* gossip mag thing! Quickly he fetched out the tracker and turned it on.

GalNav Tracker
v 10876.67
The Wagglestaff Corporation
Volans
A Galactic Maritime Board Approved Device!

Volans! That was it, they were based on Volans. Find it, and he'd find the Wagglestaff offices. Find them, and there was a good chance he'd find the *Supernova*, and if he found the *Supernova* office, he'd find Colum the Columnite! And she could tell him where toast came from. And if you knew that, you'd know where Earth was. Harry put a hand to his chin – assuming Volans was a planet and not a city, mind. Or another galaxy, for that matter. But still, it was a clue, a real clue!

He had to get off this planet somehow and get home to his mum. Oh, and along the way, get his revenge on that fish-faced freak, Gaggenow! But how? How was he going to get a spaceship, even?

Suddenly, the mound he was leaning against shifted. Harry nearly dropped his phone in surprise. A filigree of tiny cracks appeared, spreading all over the mound. A long thin crack actually split open, revealing a thin sliver of blackness, out of which dribbled a whitish slime along with a powerful smell, a bit like...what was it? Curry! That was it. Harry's stomach rumbled at the memory.

And then the mound cracked in half, spraying slime all over the place. Harry gave a short cry of shocked surprise, and fell onto his back, slapping into the mud, staring up at the mound. Two massive, powerfully muscled arms ripped out of the top, pushing it apart. Harry tried to back away, digging his heels into the ground, but to little effect, as his feet failed to get purchase in the thick mud.

The arms heaved upwards – out popped a massive head, like a human's, but big. It had a face with a button nose, and a mouth a bit like a big cat's. And eyes...no whites, just a bright aquamarine in colour, with round black pupils in the middle. It had a thick, thick neck, with a massive round chest, all of it covered in russet red fur.

Harry screamed, trying to back away, but his feet continued to flail weakly in the mud.

Then massive legs – three of them – stepped out

of the wreckage of the mound. Or rather egg, as it obviously was. It rested on its legs for a moment, massive thighs almost horizontal to its torso, and looked around. Its torso could turn almost 180 degrees, like an owl's head.

Harry blinked up at it, one hand raised in feeble defence, the other scrabbling for his multi-knife.

The…thing…noticed Harry for the first time and looked down at him. Its brow furrowed in a very human expression of puzzlement. It leaned over him, vast face a few inches from Harry's.

'Mum?' it said.

Harry blinked up at the looming giant. 'Wh-what?'

'Mum? You mother, right? Brood mother?' said the huge red-furred giant. He reached down a massive three-fingered hand. Automatically, Harry put his hand up and the…thing…or Tricrusian, it was a Tricrusian, obviously, jerked Harry to his feet, effortlessly.

'But you not look like mother,' it said. The creature looked at the other mounds. 'And why my Brood Brothers and Sisters not hatch?' As he said this, he absently broke off a bit of, well, eggshell, in effect, and began to munch it.

'You're eating…you're eating the mound,' said Harry, still not really believing what was happening.

'Yes…taste pretty bad, to be honest, but we have saying: "Instinct is there for a reason!" said the thing. He eyed Harry. 'You my mother now,' he said.

'Oh, come on, I'm not your mother!' said Harry.

'I know…but something go wrong. You Brood Mother. Brood of one, me. But there it is. Instinct,' said the thing, folding his arms.

Harry stared up at it, speechless.

'So, Mum. What next?' said the thing.

Harry stared back, still speechless. The Tricrusian looked around, gazing at the horizon.

'We must find Eater,' he said. Then it looked down at Harry. 'Though it will be hard, with only us two.'

'What do you mean, we've got to find an Eater, what are you going on about?' said Harry, finally finding some words.

'Don't you know, Mum?' said the thing.

'No, I don't know, and stop calling me Mum!' said Harry.

'I can't. You're…you're my mum,' it said.

Harry stared at the hulking beast. Maybe it was like a duckling back home on Earth. What did they call it? Imprinting. This thing had imprinted on him. Harry shook his head. Ridiculous! But then again… didn't that mean he was in charge? That it would obey him, instinctively. Look at it, it was huge and strong and it thought Harry was its mother. How cool was that?

'Well…umm, do I have to give you a first name or something?' said Harry.

'No, Ma, of course not. I'm Barl.'

'Barl? You've got a name already? But you've just hatched,' said Harry.

'Hatched out of larval stage, yes, but when I was larva, I was Barl. Now I am full adult, still Barl. You supposed to give Brood name, though. What is it?'

'Brood name?'

'Yes, you give Brood name, you know like Barl thing, or Barl…errr…thing.'

'Well, my second name is Greene – is that any good?'

'Yes, good! Barl Greene,' he said. And then he looked wistfully at the other mounds – or rather eggs. 'Barl, Greene One. Should be more Greenes, but I am premature. Anyway, Mum – why don't you know all this?'

'I think really we both know the answer to that, don't we, Barl?' said Harry, folding his arms.

'You not from around here, are you?' said Barl.

Harry shook his head. 'Nope.'

Mother and son stared at each, both with their arms folded. Then Barl blinked his aquamarine eyes at Harry and sighed, a huge sigh like the wind blowing in the trees. He unfolded his arms. 'Yes, something wrong. And now…Brood Bonded. This not good.'

They stood there for a few moments, each unsure about what to do next. Harry's legs began to wobble in the gravity.

'Barl,' he said.

'Yes, Mum?'

'Can you carry me?' said Harry.

'Sure, Ma, no problem,' said Barl, and he picked up Harry and cradled him in one huge, red-furred, muscular arm.

Harry leaned back. Barl's muscled arm was actually pretty comfortable, and he smelled of curry. Spicy curry. Harry grinned. He had a 'son'. A huge, hulking, gigantic son. That changed things – oh yes indeed. Now he could get around, make plans, do stuff.

Also, he loved curry.

23 MOTHER'S BOY

'**SO,** every egg batch has a Brood Mother assigned to it?' said Harry.

'Yes, but supposed to be a wise one, chosen by the Validators. Not a…what are you, anyway?' said Barl.

'A human. From Earth,' said Harry.

'Earth? Where that?'

'Far, far away, in another sector of the galaxy, who knows where?' said Harry wistfully.

'Ah! You an alien, then. Barl love stories about aliens!'

Harry laughed, and was about to point out that Barl was the alien, actually, but realised that wasn't true. Here, Harry was the alien.

'What happened to your other leg?' said Barl. 'Did Terrible Eater rip it off with tongue? If so, maybe Validators can re-grow it for you.'

Harry laughed again. 'No, I've only got two legs, all humans have only two.'

'Really?' said Barl. 'Weird! You like some kind of mutant. And all small and feeble too!' Then Barl frowned. 'Barl's mother is an alien. Validators, they not like this.'

Harry rubbed his jaw thoughtfully. 'We're going to have to talk to these "Validators".'

'Maybe not good idea – they not like you, I think,' said Barl.

'I don't think we've got much choice, have we? And anyway...' Harry was going to say, 'And anyway, they're my only chance of getting off this planet,' but the enormity of achieving that made him pause, not to mention the fact that Barl might not be so happy with the idea, and right now, he needed Barl.

Barl said, 'It will be difficult. We haven't even completed Rite of Resurgent Destiny.'

'Rite of what?' said Harry.

'Resurgent Destiny. Growing up. Becoming adult,' said Barl. 'Brood Mother must lead hatchlings together, hunt down and kill a Terrible Eater.'

'A Terrible Eater! Not easy, I would think, even for four or five Tricrusians,' said Harry.

'We not say Tricrusians, Hub people call us that, we call ourselves People of the Mound, or just "the People",' said Barl. 'And if you not pass the Rite, you are not citizen. You are outcast. And somehow, I don't think just you and me can hunt down and kill an Eater.'

'Oh, I don't know,' said Harry. 'But actually, we could just lie about it, couldn't we?'

'Lie? The People never lie, at least not to each other,' said Barl, shocked.

Harry frowned. 'Well...what do they do with people who don't pass the test, the outcasts, then?'

'Kill them, usually. Or maybe banishment out here in the wilds if lucky. Kind of like sentence of death anyway – very hard to live out here on own,' said Barl.

'Well, we'll just have to lie, then, because I'm not going to die out here, I can tell you that!' said Harry forcefully. Then he added, 'And nor is my son!' in what he thought was a clever twist.

'It's bad to lie, Mum. And anyway, you can't just

say, "We dunnit." You have to bring proof, a trophy, the tongue of an Eater,' said Barl.

'You mean one of those?' said Harry, pointing to the severed Eater's tongue lying in the mud nearby.

Barl's jaw dropped. 'How you get this?' he said, astonished.

Harry showed him the sergeant's sword.

'Hah! Neat,' said Barl. 'If I not see it with own eyes, Barl not believe it!'

'Your mum's pretty tough!' said Harry proudly.

'Yeah, you tough little mother! For a two-legged freak.' Then Barl made a series of short barking noises – Harry realised this was Tricrusian laughter.

'So, if we took this to your home, or town, or whatever, would it make us citizens?' said Harry.

'City of the People,' said Barl. 'And yes, if we said we did Rite together, then we be citizens.'

'Well, then, we'll just say we did, and here's the proof! Job done!' said Harry.

Barl paused, folding his arms. 'But that not true, is it? Mum did it, but not Barl. Barl not Citizen yet.'

'Oh, it's only a little lie,' said Harry. 'I mean, we have a tongue, right? That's the important thing.'

'It not good to lie. Mum should know this,' said Barl.

'Yeah, but if we don't lie – a bit – we're going to die. I mean, a mum has to look after his…her… errr…her son, right? It's my duty to take care of you, isn't it?'

Barl frowned. 'That's true…but…'

'And you wouldn't want your poor old mum to die either, would you?' said Harry.

Barl stared at the ground. 'Noooo, that true too,' he said, half convinced.

'So, when we talk to your people, you'll tell them that we completed the Rite all above board and proper, right, and here's the proof?'

'I suppose so…' said Barl miserably.

'No, you will so. This is important, Barl – I mean, son. Important. I have to know that you'll say that, or else we might as well just give up now, and start wandering the wilds. For ever.'

Barl looked around. 'Barl not like the wilds,' he said.

'Well, you know what you have to say then, right?' said Harry. 'And remember, Mummy knows best!'

Barl sighed. 'Mummy knows best, it's true,' he said. 'All right, I say we do Rite, then we become Citizens.'

'OK, cool. Now, let's get going. Where's the City of the People?'

'Over there,' said Barl, pointing beyond the Redhat Forest. He picked up the tongue, wrapping it under one arm and around his shoulders. With the other hand, he picked up Harry. And off they set, heading towards the red-hatted forest.

Beyond the forest, a wide mud plain lay before them. In the distance, a great green-capped mountain rose up to dominate the horizon.

'City of the People over there,' said Barl, pointing at the mountain. And they began sloshing across the mud plain, Barl's three-legged gait throwing up dollops of mud all over the place. It wasn't long before the fur on Barl's legs was matted with mud, as if he were wearing knee-high boots of brown sludge.

Harry looked up at Barl. 'Is it true that the Tricrusians…errr…the People, I mean, have technology? Advanced technology, you know, like space travel?' he said.

'Oh yes,' said Barl. 'We very advanced.'

Harry narrowed his eyes. Didn't seem like it – Barl was naked, after all, and didn't seem to have anything at all in terms of tech. 'But you…you don't have, well, even a stick or anything,'

Barl looked down at Harry, his expression clearly saying 'What are you, stupid, or something?'

'I just got out of an egg, course I don't have anything!' said Barl. 'And the Rite has to be done naturally, with only tools that can be made by hand.'

'Just to make it that little bit harder, eh?' said Harry with a grin.

'Yes, just a little. So, Mum better not mention her sword! It smells of Hub tech. No, you used your brains, made yourself bait, lured Eater in, I sprang out and ambushed it with blade made from Redhat tree bark, yes?'

'Absolutely, my son, good thinking!' said

Harry, though being called 'her' made him a tad uncomfortable. Still, best not point out that he was in fact a he. That could cause problems.

'And you're sure about the space travel?' said Harry, still not really believing it.

'Yes, yes, Mum! Why, you wanna leave the Mound?' Barl said, half-jokingly.

'Maybe,' said Harry noncommittally.

Barl frowned. 'Barl must go wherever Mother go, but Barl not want to leave planet, Mound is his home.'

They fell silent for a time, each with his own thoughts.

Tirelessly, Barl strode on, eating up the miles, bringing the huge mountain in the distance ever closer. Harry noticed that his fur was actually heating up slightly. It gave off a spicy odour, like chillies frying in a pan. It was starting to make Harry's eyes water.

'What's with your fur, Barl? It's kind of sizzling,' said Harry.

'Getting energy from sun,' said Barl absently, as if that were perfectly natural.

Amazing, really, Harry thought to himself. Smelt good too, but it was getting painful on his eyes. He took out his flask.

'Mornin', Harry, my little darling,' said the flask. 'What can I do for you? Let me take a little guess, you're thirsty, right, and you want me to fire up my big ol' Atmospheric Distillers, just for you, honey?'

Barl's head recoiled in surprise.

'Little AI. In the flask. You know, computer?' said Harry, pointing at the HydroPal.

Barl looked a little miffed at that. 'Barl know about computers. Barl not stupid,' he said.

'Oh, OK,' said Harry, taking a big swig, and then pouring some over his head and eyes.

That really helped with the 'frying chilli' effect.

'Oooh, that was fun,' said the HydroPal.

Harry offered a drink to Barl. He nodded, and they came to a halt. He put Harry down, and picked up the HydroPal. 'Oh my, you're a big one!' it squealed. Barl put the flask to his lips, drained it dry, and handed it back.

'Well, I never,' said the HydroPal. 'He's a thirsty boy, ain't he? Now I'll be Distilling water all day long!'

Harry raised his eyes. If she went on like this all the time, she'd start getting on his nerves.

'You hungry?' said Harry to Barl.

'Barl always hungry!' was the reply. 'What you got, Mum?'

Harry reached into his pack and brought out a jar of Nutrit Porridge. He scooped out a dollop and began to munch on it listlessly, before handing it over to Barl.

Barl took a sniff, dipped in a massive finger and sucked some porridge off it.

'YEEUKKK!' he yelped, and spat it out. 'That disgusting!'

'I know,' said Harry, 'but that's all we've got and you've got to keep your strength up – sunlight isn't going to be enough! Now eat up, there's a good boy.'

'But Barl hate it!' he wailed.

'Eat your porridge, and stop whining,' said Harry,

grinning. He was getting into this 'Mum' business. He realised what his mum must have gone through all those years trying to get him to do stuff. He felt a pang of loss as he thought of her.

Meanwhile, Barl's shoulders slumped. 'Yes, Mum,' he said, as he slurped out the jar and gulped it down as fast as he could in an attempt to get it over with as quickly as possible, just like Harry used to do with Christmas Brussels sprouts.

Just then, the sergeant said, 'Motion detected, five hundred metres ahead.'

Harry froze. Barl put a hand up to shield his eyes and examined the horizon.

'It's not an Eater, is it?' said Harry.

'No, Mum, it's Wildwatchers,' said Barl. He rubbed his jaw, a worried look on his face, just like a human.

'Wildwatchers?' said Harry.

'Yeah, the Wildwatch. All People must serve in Wildwatch at some time. Patrol the Wild, make sure Eaters don't get into the City, check up on Brood Eggs, Solar Plants, that kind of thing.'

'So they're the People?' said Harry. 'Coming this way?'

Barl nodded. 'They detect us,' he said.

'Well…that's good, isn't it? They'll take us to the City, right?' said Harry.

Barl looked at Harry. 'Maybe. Depends,' he said.

'Depends on what?'

Barl shrugged. 'Who they are. What we say. What they think of you. That kind of thing.'

'Well, yeah, but how bad could it be?' said Harry.

'Very bad. Maybe they just kill us.'

24 THREE'S A CROWD

A vehicle began to draw near at quite a lick. Its engines gave a low thrumming hum. It looked a bit like a huge trike, with three massive wheels, really broad and wide, good for getting traction in all this mud. In between the wheels rested a big triangular cab. Its front was made entirely of glass, with the rest of it coated in bright, shining silvery stuff. Probably solar panels, thought Harry, as the Tricrusian sun was so strong.

Harry looked up at Barl. He stood there waiting, the Eater's tongue wrapped around one shoulder, his other hand a clenched fist on his hip, torso puffed out, full of bravado. You had to admire his courage! Harry realised he felt proud, as if Barl really was his son, somehow.

Ridiculous! Harry grinned, in a kind of nervous way, as the trike came to a halt. The front screen

rose up with a hydraulic hiss, and out stepped three Tricrusians. They too were red-furred, three-legged, two-armed, cat-faced giants, but there the similarity ended. Each had heavy, leathery boots on their legs. They wore brightly coloured loincloths, and harnesses over their torsos, with pockets and pouches and buckles and clasps off which hung various tools. Devices were strapped to their massive arms, and they wore complex headgear with earphones, microphones, antennae and so on. Each leg had stuff strapped to it. On their backs were what looked like classic alien blasters of some kind. In other words, they were teched up to the max, whilst also leaving large areas of fur open to the sun to get energy.

OK then, thought Harry. *Here we go. Live or die.*

Everyone stood for a moment, in silence, each examining the other. Harry began to notice little differences. The one in the middle had a tall hat, a bit like a top hat, but made of some kind of metal, with a little satellite type dish on top. It looked very silly indeed. Harry tried not to laugh.

The one on the left had a blue headband on, with a smiley cat face on it. That was almost too much for Harry – he had to put a hand up to stifle a laugh.

And the one on the right…the others wore knee-high boots, but this one wore bright yellow, purple-dotted stockings all the way up to its bright yellow loincloth.

That really was too much for Harry and he laughed out loud, pointing at the stockings – he just couldn't help himself. The long-stockinged alien growled, and drew forth its gun, aiming it at Harry. Harry stopped laughing, cursing himself for a fool.

The Tricrusian with the top hat, the one in the middle, put out a hand, calming things down.

'Is that you, Barl?' he said.

'It is, Chief Watcher Throgs,' said Barl. 'But now I am Barl Greene One.'

The one called Throgs, with the silly top hat, turned to look at the one with the yellow stockings. They exchanged an enigmatic look, and then Throgs turned back to Barl.

'You're not supposed to be out yet. Where's the rest of your Brood?'

'Unhatched,' Barl said.

The other three gasped. Harry noticed the smiley face on the headband. It wasn't smiling any more; rather it'd changed to an expression of astonished horror, two paws raised up to either side of the face. The Tricrusian's actual face remained impassive.

'And the eggs?' said Chief Watcher Throgs.

'Fine, fine,' said Barl, 'they'll hatch normal time soon, don't worry.'

Harry stared at the headband in fascination. The face had changed to an exaggerated expression of relief, a paw resting on its forehead.

Then the one in the yellow stockings spoke.

'And this? What is this?' she said. But her voice came out really high-pitched and squeaky, as if she'd just breathed in a balloonful of helium.

Harry simply couldn't help himself, and he started to giggle nervously again. Mostly out of fear, but also because the situation was kind of surreal – after all, she had a high-pitched squeaky voice and wore yellow stockings with purple polka dots.

'Listen to it! It is some kind of vermin, we should destroy it, now,' squeaked the yellow-stockinged Tricrusian, raising her gun to fire.

'Hold!' said Throgs. 'Put that Carbine down!'

The yellow-stockinged one paused for a moment, as if she were thinking about shooting anyway.

'Squeaker Longstockings!' said Throgs. 'Put that gun down now – that's an order!'

Squeaker Longstockings? You've got to be kidding me, Harry thought to himself, and he sank to his knees, trying not to laugh and laugh and laugh until everything was better.

'Don't shoot, please,' said Barl, taking a step forward.

Squeaker glared at Barl but she did lower her gun. 'All right, as it's you, Barl,' she trilled.

Throgs folded his arms, as if in irritation. 'Well, whatever,' he said. 'But there'll be no killing until I give the order, all right?'

'I'm sorry,' said Harry, and then he began to blabber in a nervous rush of panic. 'I'm so sorry, I'm just really scared, I got lost here, don't know where I am, this planet is so weird, then there was an exploding egg and I met Barl, and he's got three legs, and there were these flying red hats, and stinky mud, and nice curry, and green clouds, and last night this…'

'Shut up, Mum, you say nonsense!' said Barl.

The other three froze in shock. The smiley face became a shocked face, with all its fur standing on end. The Tricrusian's actual face remained still, like it was carved from stone.

'Did you just say what I think you said?' said Throgs in shock.

Barl nodded sheepishly.

'But I was supposed to be brood mother!' wailed Squeaker.

'Unfortunately, this came along,' said Barl, waving a hand at Harry.

Squeaker Longstockings screwed up her face in anger. 'Abomination!' she said, and raised her gun to fire again. Harry raised his hands in a futile gesture of defence.

'No!' cried Barl. 'Don't kill my mum!'

Squeaker paused, blinking.

'It's an alien!' said Throgs. 'Your mum's an alien – it's an Abomination!'

Squeaker nodded, aiming again.

'You'll have to kill me too,' said Barl, lumbering forward.

Squeaker frowned, unsure. The third one, Smiley Face, just stood there, impassive.

Throgs said, 'Technically, we should kill you. Brood Bond with an outsider? Abomination, it's quite clear, even if it's not your fault.'

Harry found himself staring down the barrel of an alien blaster. Was this it? After all he'd been through, to be gunned down in the mud like some kind of verminous rat?

'Wait!' said the third Tricrusian, his smiley face showing an expression of curious surprise.

Squeaker flicked her bright blue eyes over, finger poised on the trigger.

'What is it, Stoneface?' said Throgs.

Stoneface simply pointed to Barl, his smiley face grinning madly. 'Eater tongue,' he said.

Throgs stared at it. 'Oh yeah,' he said after a second or two. 'The Rite...surely not! Just the two of you?'

Barl didn't say anything. He simply hefted the Eater's tongue, and held it out, showing it to them.

'It's still an Abomination,' hissed Squeaker.

'Yeah, but if they've done the Rite... Well, now they're citizens. Technically. Sort of. Or something,' said Throgs.

'Validators,' said Stoneface.

'Yeah, you're right, Stoneface, we'll take 'em back.

Let the Council decide,' said Throgs.

'What? No! We should just kill them now – get it done,' said Squeaker.

'Not up to us. Now, get them up into the Mud Tracker, and let's go,' said Throgs.

Squeaker Longstockings blinked. 'Bah,' she said, holstering her gun. 'The Validators will sentence them to death anyway.'

'Maybe so, but that's their decision, not ours,' said Throgs. 'Now mount up and let's get going!'

Harry staggered over to the Mud Tracker. He'd survived once again by the skin of his teeth. Though, really, this could just as easily be an 'out of the frying pan and into the fire' type situation.

Barl helped him up. The interior of the Tracker had a big driver's seat, and then huge benches along the two side walls. It was bit like being inside an enormous metal wigwam. Harry and Barl were chained up in one corner, though Harry could have easily slipped the manacles they'd put on his wrists, they were so large. But what was the point? He could barely walk in this gravity, and in any case, where would he go? Squeaker and Stoneface sat on

the benches to either side of Barl and Harry, whilst Throgs sat in the driver's seat.

The Mud Tracker took off with a growling hum, its wheels powering them on through the mud like a dolphin through water. Suspension was poor, though, and they were bumped around all over the place. Well, Harry was, anyway.

Squeaker Longstockings took out a knife; to Harry it was more like a sword. She began to sharpen it on a whetstone, staring at Harry the whole time with her bright blue eyes. Harry tried to concentrate on the view outside the front windscreen, but her stare was intimidating and distracting. He kept glancing back at her, making sure she wasn't about to run him through or something. She grinned every time he did so. Every now and again, she'd thrust her knife at him playfully or mime cutting him up.

Harry hated to be intimidated, hated to be scared… After a while, he'd had enough. He had to do something. Anything! He snuck a hand into his backpack, grabbed the sergeant, waited for a particularly bumpy section of mud, and whilst everyone was distracted, whispered, 'Survivor Mode'. Then he waited for Squeaker to look away, flicked on the multi-knife's lighter, leaned forward and down ever so slightly, and set fire to one of her stockings.

Nothing happened for a moment, and then suddenly she squealed in shocked surprise. Small flames licked up one massive calf. Desperately, she dropped her knife, and started batting out the flames with her massive hands.

Harry grinned. Stoneface's smiley face showed a big grin too; he'd obviously enjoyed that. Squeaker's face turned into a mask of rage. She grabbed Harry round the throat and slammed him back against the far wall with ferocious force.

Harry's head began to swim, and he almost passed out there and then from the impact. Barl shouted, struggling to intervene, but the manacles kept him at bay. Squeaker raised her other hand to smash Harry's head in – but then Throgs shouted, 'Enough! Get a hold of yourself, Longstockings, or I'll have you charged with Disobedience!'

Squeaker's face was inches from Harry's, her blue eyes blazing, her chicken vindaloo breath all over Harry. She paused. Harry scrabbled at her hand ineffectually. He couldn't breathe. Then she loosened her grip and let Harry slide back down onto the bench.

'Bah, you're not worth it,' she muttered as she leaned back, and folded her arms.

Ahead, the green-capped mountain loomed

larger and larger, until it filled the windscreen completely.

'Where's this city, then?' said Harry.

'Inside mountain,' said Stoneface.

'The People hollow it out,' added Barl.

Harry could see now that the mountain was covered in thousands and thousands of windows and doors, leading onto a host of balconies, galleries and walkways, carved out of the mountainside. As they approached on a road of hardened mud, great doors opened leading to a vast interior space, where all manner of vehicles were parked, from single-seater open-air trikes, to vast multi-wheeled trucks.

From there, they were dragged in chains by the Wildwatch patrol to an enormous elevator. This shot up at such a rate that the G-force pressed Harry to the ground, where he lay gasping like a fish out of water, much to Squeaker Longstockings's amusement.

Harry began to hate her with every fibre of his being – more than he hated Gaggenow, if that were possible. As he glared up at her, Barl leaned down and cradled Harry in his arms.

Squeaker sneered at this. 'Disgusting,' she muttered.

'Don't worry, Mum,' said Barl, almost tenderly. 'Lift only last a few seconds.' And so it did, for moments later it came to a shuddering halt and the doors swept open.

'Welcome to the Hall of the Validators,' said Throgs.

BARL and Harry were bundled forward. Up ahead, a vast window, at least a hundred feet wide and fifty feet high, looked down upon the plains and a Redhat forest that marched away to the horizon. It looked to Harry as if ten thousand red-hatted Chinese peasants kneeled in silent worship at the foot of the mountain.

Before the window was a long table behind which three more Tricrusians waited, seated on tall stool-like structures, their three legs hanging down, booted feet resting in curious-looking stirrups. Harry stared around the huge hall. The walls were adorned with what Harry took to be works of art: triangular framed paintings; images; sculptures of all sorts. The floor appeared to be of baked plains-mud, inlaid with glittering metallic lacework.

'Come forward,' said the middle Tricrusian, his

voice booming, amplified in some way. 'I am Efour, the High Validator.' Barl and Harry stepped up to a square of patterned Redhat bark, to stand before the Validators. Just behind them stood Stoneface, Throgs and Squeaker Longstockings.

The High Validator wore another one of those top hats, this time with what looked like a golden orb on top, floating a few inches above it. He gestured to his left and said, 'And this is Moggs, Validator of the Right.' Moggs also wore a metal top hat, this one crowned with a floating triangle, bright red in colour. Efour turned to his right, the golden orb turning perfectly in time. 'And this is Flixnix, Validator of the Left,' said the High Validator. Flixnix's hat had a blue floating square on top.

Harry stared up at them. Yellow stockings, animated smileys, left is right, right is left, cats in hats with floating... Argh, this place was doing his head in!

'So, we have a bit of an...oddness, I see,' said Efour, the High Validator. 'You have Brood Bonded with an alien? Is that correct?'

'Yeah, 'fraid so,' said Harry.

'Not you, idiot, him!' said Moggs, the Validator of the Right, pointing a three-fingered hand at Barl.

'Oh, right, yeah, of course,' mumbled Harry.

'Well, Barl, is it true?' said Efour, the High Validator.

'Yes, Highness,' said Barl humbly.

'Well, Barl, where is this creature from?' said the High Validator.

'He is from somewhere called...umm, Soil, I think Mum say.'

'Soil? As in soiled, you know, like a nappy?' said Moggs, the Validator of the Right.

Harry interrupted, irritated by people always getting the name of his planet wrong, 'No, no, not Soil. Earth. As in the ground, the earth, but we call the whole planet that.'

'So, you're confirming you're from another planet, that's what you're saying, right? An alien?' said Flixnix.

'Well, yes, I guess so,' said Harry.

'Are you from the Hub?' asked Efour.

'I bet he was sent here as a spy, to steal our mud – you know how much they want it!' trilled Squeaker Longstockings. 'Kill it, I say, kill it!'

'No, no,' said Harry. 'I'm not from the Hub, I was kidnapped by Greys from my own planet, and then the Leptira…'

'THE LEPTIRA!' screamed Squeaker Longstockings, her voice reaching painfully high levels. 'It'll bring the Leptira down upon us, we must destroy it for the Abomination it is and to save ourselves!'

'Please, Squeaker, please, calm yourself. We must at least find out what the curious little creature has to say,' said the High Validator.

'Indeed. Even though it's as ugly as an Eater's bum, the Way demands it,' added Moggs.

Squeaker looked up, and folded her arms in frustration. 'Bah, kill it, kill it now,' she muttered loudly.

'Enough!' said the High Validator. 'Now...errr...thing...'

'Harry – Captain Harry,' said Harry, his heart hammering. He had to get this right, everything rested on it.

'Ha-Ree, yes, go on,' said Efour.

Harry gulped. 'We fought the Leptira off,' he said, glancing at Squeaker, 'and lost them. But then my crew marooned me here, tricked me.'

'Marooned, eh? What did you do to make your crew turn against you?' said Flixnix the Validator of the Left, leaning forward.

'I didn't do anything, it was Gaggenow!' said Harry, cursing himself for his lack of tact and diplomatic skills. He'd made himself look bad, and that wasn't going to help in winning them over. 'He plotted against me, wanted to take over the ship.' Harry closed his eyes. That was going to sound like paranoid madness too. This wasn't going well.

'Not a very trustworthy species, then, you humans from Soiled,' said Moggs.

'Earth. And Gaggenow's not human, he's an Ichthysupial,' said Harry, his heart sinking. He was really screwing this up.

'Ah…' said Efour. The other two Validators nodded knowingly. 'We have had dealings with them before,' continued Efour.

'That makes sense, then,' said Moggs. 'An Ichthysupial. Hah!'

'Well, whatever,' said Flixnix. 'Perhaps he is telling the truth, and it's not the creature's fault it is here. But still, it has Mothered one of ours, and that is an Abomination! Not only that, it has brought its Brood back without completing the Rite. That too is a crime. We should destroy it, and Barl too.'

'Actually,' said Barl, 'we have an Eater tongue. Throgs has it in the Tracker hold.'

The three Validators stared in shock for a moment.

'Is this true, Chief Watcher?' said Efour.

Throgs nodded. 'True,' he said.

'What, just Barl and this…this little legless whatsit?' said Flixnix.

'Well, actually,' began Barl, 'what really happened…OW!' Barl looked down. Harry was roughly pulling out some of Barl's fur. He glared up at Barl. Barl stared back.

'Well?' said Efour, frowning.

Barl looked up. 'Umm,' he said, shifting his weight, before going on, 'umm…yes, we kill Eater. Between us. My mum very clever, trick Eater, and Barl kill it.'

'Gah! They are Citizens, then,' said Moggs, throwing his hands up.

The High Validator nodded slowly. 'Well, that's a glibberdee dibble, and no mistake,' he said.

Harry tapped the translator in his ear.

'"Glibberdee dibble", a phrase denoting unusual

circumstance. "A pretty pickle" is a close Earth approximation, though dibble means "odorous" and a Glibberdee is a kind of nut, so a literal translation would be "Stinking Peanut", explained the translator.

'Stinking Peanut, indeed,' said Moggs, gazing at the floor in thought. 'We can't just execute them out of hand because they are citizens and haven't committed a crime.'

'Abomination, though – that's a crime, surely,' said Squeaker Longstockings shrilly.

'No, not really. Technically speaking it's a Heresy, not a crime,' said Efour, stroking his chin.

'And we can't accept them into the City, as they are an Abomination,' said Flixnix.

'Exile, then?' said Moggs.

'Another Stinking Peanut,' said Efour. 'Exile is only for those Citizens who have committed a crime – you see, the problem is nobody's ever been an Abomination and a Citizen before!'

'A mission, then!' piped up Harry.

'A…what?' said the Validators together.

'A mission! We're Citizens, right, an official Brood

and that. Brood Greene, or whatever. Presumably you can command us to do tasks and things, for the City, right?'

'Well, yes, sometimes,' said Efour.

'OK, then, so give us a mission...off world,' said Harry.

The Validators stared.

'Off world...' said Efour. 'Yes, yes, that would work!'

Moggs and Flixnix nodded in agreement.

'Nooo!' said Squeaker. 'NOOOOO!!! They have to die,' she shrieked.

'For the last time, SHUT UP, Longstockings, or you'll find that it's you who's an exile!' said the High Validator angrily.

Harry hurried on. 'You could send us out to scout nearby stars and worlds, to explore the Hub, find out what they really think of you, how powerful they are, how much they want your...umm...the mud, or whatever – all that stuff could be invaluable to you!'

'That's true...' said Efour, nodding thoughtfully.

'We don't even have to come back, we can send

monthly reports by Galnet or whatever, you needn't see us ever again!' said Harry enthusiastically.

'But Barl not want to leave the Mound!' said Barl.

'Barl not have much choice,' muttered Squeaker from behind.

'Quite so,' said Efour, 'And anyway, technically, you'll be part of the first galactic expedition ever sent by the People. It's a big honour.'

'Exile is an honour?' said Barl bitterly.

'Well, you can't stay here, and that's that. This way, at least you're not officially exiled, and still a Citizen. You should be grateful,' said Efour.

'Suppose so,' said Barl, looking down and sweeping away an imaginary bit of dust with his front foot.

Harry looked behind him. Squeaker was glaring at him, one hand on the dagger strapped to a massive, yellow-stockinged thigh. Harry grinned at her, and stuck out his tongue. Squeaker's eyes widened so much, Harry thought they'd explode. Suddenly her fur changed colour just for a second, a flash of angry blue, and she stepped toward Harry menacingly.

'Right, that's it,' said Efour. 'Throgs, Stoneface, grab Squeaker and get her out of here, now!!!'

'Sir,' said Throgs. Stoneface and Throgs took Squeaker by an arm, and began to drag her to the door. Harry smiled at her and doffed an imaginary cap. Longstockings, braced in the arms of Throgs and Stoneface, stared back, mouthing words at him. Something about 'hanging some bunting up to celebrate his departure...' Or was it hunting? And then hanging? He couldn't be sure. Harry turned back, grinning hugely. He could hardly believe it

– this was turning out better than he could have possibly hoped for.

'So, an expedition. A diplomatic mission. Fact-finding, that kind of thing...what ships have we got, Moggs?' said Efour.

'Well, I think a Space Tracker – it's the smallest and cheapest we have. Designed for a crew of three. Has a Sundrive.'

'Yes, that should do nicely,' said Efour.

'They'll need supplies too,' said Flixnix.

'No problem there. But what about money? Won't they need some of that Hub money...what do they call it?' said Efour.

'Galactic Credits! Don't worry, I have some of that,' said Harry, holding up his Credit Chips. 'Not much, though...'

'Hmm, well, we can fill the hold with some of those rare metals the Hub want so much. You can trade that, maybe,' suggested Moggs helpfully.

Harry nodded enthusiastically. 'Thank you, thank you, we won't let you down, I promise!' he said. Now he could go after Gaggenow and the girls – get his ship back. His other ship! And then he could find Volans and Colum the Columnite; maybe she'd be able to tell him where earth was, and he could go straight home. Find his mum. What would his mum make of Barl, though? And would they let him take Barl to school? Questions, questions!

In the meantime, he'd do as the Tricrusians asked as well, of course. Why not? He was a Tricrusian Brood Mother after all… Harry chuckled.

'So, then, Brood Greene. You shall undertake an Exploratory Mission of unspecified length and duration. Your task is to collect information for the People. You will also represent the People, so conduct yourselves with all due decorum, honour and general all-round decency, as befits your station. Well, that last bit really applies to Barl. Probably best not to mention you're a Citizen at all, really, Harry, if you can help it,' said Efour.

Harry grinned a big, happy grin.

26 A SHOT IN THE DARK

HARRY lay back in the blast-off position, strapped into the Motherseat. Beside him sat Barl, in the Engineerseat. To his right, a third seat remained empty, the Battleseat. They would have to avoid combat wherever possible. The *Greene One*, as they'd named the ship, didn't have a computer – well, an AI that is – not in the way that the *Fartface Banana Nose* did. It had computers, of course, but not intelligent ones, not ones you could tell to do stuff for you. Everything had to be done by Barl and Harry. They'd been given a crash course in flying Space Trackers, using a bit of Tricrusian technology called Narcosaturation. Basically, your brain was taught stuff whilst you slept. Harry wanted to learn other stuff like PanGal, but it was really designed for Tricrusians, and the flying course alone had given Harry terrible headaches,

so he'd had to make do with the flying.

The three seats were tightly packed into a really bright-looking cockpit full of instruments, readouts and coloured switches and buttons, designed for Tricrusian hands, so they were big and chunky like a toddler's toy.

Behind them, a short corridor led to a kind of communal galley area for food preparation and recreation. Beyond that were three sleeping cabins and three smallish cargo holds, and then the Sundrive and the engines. The whole ship rested on three stout legs, and looked from the outside pretty much like a 1950s style space rocket. All in all, it was much smaller and much less sophisticated than the *Fartface Banana Nose*.

'Engaging Planetary Escape Shield,' said Barl, flicking a switch above his head.

Because gravity was so strong on the planet, it took a lot of effort to get a ship up into space, out of what they called the Gravity Well. The Tricrusians had a novel solution – the *Greene One* had been loaded into what was in effect a huge gun or cannon. Basically, they were going to be shot out into space – by a nuclear bomb exploding under their feet.

It sounded totally bonkers to Harry when he first heard it, but apparently it was tried and tested and worked every time. Then, once they were in space, each of the three legs would open up like umbrellas, turning into massive magnetic solar sails. The *Greene One* would then sail the solar wind, supplemented by a kind of Ion Drive engine, set in between the three solar sail legs.

And then...the Sun Drive. This was even more

bonkers! They would have to sail right into the outer corona of the sun, protected by something called a 'Heliobturator'. Once inside the sun, they could 'jump' instantly to another nearby sun – in this case, Haddus Prime, as Harry's GalNav Tracker had that as the last known position of the *Fartface Banana Nose*. It would be a good place to start.

'Initiating Nuclear Meltdown,' said Harry, hitting a big red button over his head.

'This is Launch Control,' said a voice over the radio. 'Nuclear Countdown begins in…three, two, one, go! One minute, and counting.'

Harry stared up at the small patch of yellow sky at the end of the firing tube. He looked over at Barl. Barl looked back and smiled.

'Don't worry, Mum,' he said. 'Everything OK.'

Harry smiled back. Here he was on the cusp of another adventure. And this time he had a huge furry red alien for a son. What would his mum think?

'Fifty seconds and counting,' said Launch Control.

'Engaging Kinetic Dampeners,' said Harry,

flicking a switch – well, more like a lever to him.

'Forty seconds and counting,' said Launch Control.

'Engaging Gravity Dampeners,' said Harry, pulling another lever. Instantly, the heavy burden of the Mound's gravity was eased. They'd come to a compromise on that – it was half gravity for Barl, but still fifty per cent more than Earth gravity for Harry, but it was much more bearable. He could actually walk in that. If it wasn't for the Gravity Dampeners, the G-forces released from being blasted into space would have killed him anyway.

'Thirty seconds and counting,' said Launch Control.

Harry wondered what Gaggenow and the twins were up to. Had the girls missed him? Hah! Not likely. Well, maybe Bet. A bit. What would they think if they knew that he was coming after them? With a big hulking friend, too.

'Twenty seconds and counting,' said Launch Control.

And when he did find them – and he would find them, oh yes! Well, there'd be a reckoning then –

that Gaggenow had it coming. He had Harry's ship, and Harry wanted it back. And once he'd got that, he'd go to Volans, find out where Earth was, and get back to his mum.

'Ten seconds and counting,' said Launch Control.

Harry nestled back into the cushioned safety of the Motherseat, especially built for him.

'Three, two, one, fire!' yelled Launch Control.

There was a vast explosion that filled the tube with fire and smoke – Harry felt as if it he'd been tossed into the air like a tennis ball and whacked as hard as hard could be by some kind of gigantic tennis racket of the gods. He was slammed back into his chair. He couldn't breathe. For a moment he thought the People's engineers had got their calculations wrong, and he was going to die after all, but soon the pressure eased and he gasped in a lungful of air.

Suddenly, they were in space. Ahead: only stars, a vast array of stars, forever twinkling in the endless dark, a wonderful, liberating sight for Harry.

'Barl, set a course for the sun,' said Harry.

'Yes, Mum!' said Barl.

He'd checked the ship's navigation computers – nothing in there about Volans or the Wagglestaff Corporation or where they might be. All he had to go on about anything was the last known position of the *Fartface Banana Nose* – and that was Haddus Prime.

Harry smiled. It was good to be out here once more, to be a Starship Captain again.

And he'd done it. Against all the odds, he'd got off the planet. Eat that, Gaggs! Next stop, Gaggenow

and the girls. And then Volans and home.

Down below on the planet's surface, unnoticed by the crew of *Greene One*, a flash of light marked the launch of another ship…

About the Author

Jamie Thomson has lived in a world of his own for some time now. He claims to get messages beamed to him from outer space, sent by a young man from earth who was kidnapped by aliens and who is now lost somewhere on the wrong side of the galaxy, and that the whole story is actually true.

Riiight... Personally, I think the author's totally bonkers, but hey. Whatever.

Oh, and he also wrote the *Dark Lord* series of books and won the Roald Dahl Funny Prize in 2012. (Definitely bonkers then!) And he has a website if you want to know more about his crazy stories:

www.jamiethomson.com

Acknowledgements

I would like to thank the Galactic News Network and the Wagglestaff Corporation of the planet Volans, for their invaluable aid in providing me with a Quantum Receiver, so I could unscramble Harry's intergalactic text messages and emails.

Also, my pal, Dave Morris, for finding Harry's messages in the first place. He's a bit of a science whizz is my mate Dave. Though actually I think he might be an alien with a holo-harness in fact, just like Gaggenow. I mean, how else could he know so much about space and stuff? Also, his face is a bit fishy-looking, just like Gaggenow's.

Oh, and Megan Larkin at Orchard, for doing such a good job of helping me transcribe Harry's logs. Come to think of it, she may be an alien too. They're everywhere, you know! Other useful aliens: Arvind Shah for doing such a good job with the layout and stuff. Rosie McIntosh, my alien editor. Jamie

Lenman, not for doing all the pictures (although they are brill) but mostly for having such a good name. Matthew Britton, the art alien, for doing such a great cover.

And finally, my long-suffering partner Lucy, who has been desperately trying to get back to her home planet for ages but I won't let her go.

Jamie Thomson
July 2014

Read on for a sneak peek at
Jamie Thomson's hilarious

The Fall

'AAAaaaaaaaaarrrrrrrrrrrrggggggggghhhhhhhh!'

His fall seemed to go on forever. It felt like bits of him were being stripped away, as if he was changing into something else as he fell. After a long time his cries of rage and fear faded and he sank into a kind of sleep, all sensation lost, falling silently in an immense void of nothingness for what seemed like an eternity. Then, suddenly

KA-RUNCH!!!!

Pain, so much pain... Then it faded away and he took in a great shuddering gulp of air. He coughed and spat out a glob of black mucus. He watched as the mucus formed a small puddle of shiny black oil. He lay for a while, just breathing.

The ground felt like hard gravel. He could barely move. He couldn't think properly and he felt weak and listless. The sky above was blue, painfully blue.

He hated blue skies and sunlight.

He needed help. He called out for his lieutenant, Dread Gargon, Hewer of Limbs, but his voice caught in his throat. He tried again.

'Gaa… Gargon, to me!' he tried to bellow in his most commanding tones, but it only came out as a little squeak, high-pitched and boyish. Where was the dark, imperious voice that sent forth his Legions of Dread to bloody war and pitiless plunder?

He tried once more, but again it came out as a high-pitched trill. He groaned and tried raising his head, but couldn't. He wondered whether his Helm of the Hosts of Hell had slipped off again – if it wasn't balanced just right it could catch his neck in an uncomfortable pinch.

He reached up, but there was no Helm at all. He couldn't feel any horns either, or knobbly ridges of bone, only what seemed like a brown mop of hair on a rather small head. And his teeth! They didn't feel right either – no tusks or yellowed fangs to inspire terror and dread. Instead his head felt like a little human head, just like the ones he usually kept impaled on those iron spikes over the Gates of

Doom, or the ones that Gargon wore hanging from his belt.

What was going on and where was Gargon?

There was something else as well. Too much harsh sunlight usually fried his undead flesh like an egg in a pan, but he couldn't feel the usual sunfire burns. Not only that, the sky actually seemed rather beautiful. White clouds drifted serenely across the bright blue canopy of the heavens, and birds sang songs of joy in nearby trees. The sun warmed him nicely and a feeling of…hmmm, let's see now, something he hadn't felt in aeons, a sense of… peace came over him! Yes, that was it. A sense of peace. How could that be? He'd spent years trying to perfect a spell to cover the sky in The Black Vapours of Gloom but now the bright blueness didn't seem to bother him.

A wash of pain came over him again. That's better, he thought. He didn't want to feel a sense of peace. It just wasn't the sort of thing he should be feeling. After all, he had his reputation to consider…

With a great effort he was able to turn his head a little and take his eyes off the sky. He saw a low building of dull grey stone on his left, squat and unsightly. Excellent. At least someone was making ugly stuff around here. Maybe it was of Orcish design. You could always rely on Orcs to make ugly stuff.

He saw some kind of banner flying over the building. Runes were written on it, in a strange language. To his surprise he realised he could read them. 'Saveco Supermarket' it said. A market. That didn't sound Orcish. Orcs tended to prefer pillaging to shopping. And Saveco – was he the local overlord, perhaps? Lord Saveco, Smiter of Foes, the Pitiless One? Something about it didn't sound right.

He looked the other way. What he saw was even stranger to his eyes. Several rows of oddly shaped metal boxes gleamed in the sunlight. They were of all kinds of different colours, and glass plates had been set into their sides. They rested on four wheels, thickly encrusted with some kind of black resin that looked like the hard-set mucus of the Giant Spiderbeasts of Skorpulos. One of the boxes suddenly shuddered into life, rattling away with a terrible noise like the coughing shriek of the dragon before it discharged its fiery breath.

He tried to bend the box to his will. If it was a thing of evil, it should instinctively follow his command. 'Beast of Steel and Mucus – I command you in the Name of the Dark Lord and by the Power of the Nine Hells!'

But his voice came out as a querulous squeak. The metal box moved away as if he hadn't even spoken. Then he noticed what looked like a human woman inside the box, peering out through the glass panels. Of course! It was some kind of horseless chariot, driven no doubt by magic. The woman must be a potent witch indeed to command such a thing. The wizardry of mortals was getting sophisticated and powerful. He'd have to watch them more closely.

Then he heard a voice – another human by the sound of it – shouting, 'Hey, are you all right, lad?'

Buy these books or endure my eternal wrath!
Yours insincerely, Dirk Lloyd

978 1 40831 511 8 Pbk
978 1 40831 655 9 eBook

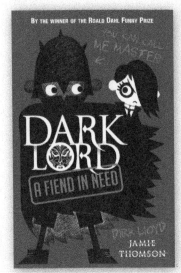

978 1 40831 512 5 Pbk
978 1 40831 656 6 eBook

978 1 40833 025 8 Pbk
978 1 40833 028 9 eBook